LET ME FIND OUT

TERRANCE HOWARD

CHAPTER 1

"ANOTHER DAY"
(GLASS HOUSE)

The afternoon sunlight beamed down upon the sharp razor wire which occupied the top of a twelve-foot-high chain link fence. The barrier surrounded one of the oldest correctional facilities in the state of Texas. There, sat the humongous red brick, four tier building covered with several hundred thousand individual windowpanes. The prison was better known as The Glass House.

Windows were busted out wherever you looked, or either covered with years of grime and dirt to the point you couldn't see in or out.

Beyond the concrete walls and steel bars extracurricular activity was taking place inside of a storage room closet on one of the administrative segregation cell blocks.

"Ooooo! Yeah that's it. Mmmmm. Mmmmm. Suck that dick. Sssss...Ahhh," he moaned quietly as he strained his hearing listening for any movement down the row. "Turn around and pull your pants down. Bend over and spread that ass," he ordered, gazing out the door as his dick throbbed up and down.

"I never fucked nobody in the ass before. Oooo Weee, this ass is tight. Oooo, Oooo, Ohhhh," he grunted loudly not hearing his name being called because he was lost in the moment.

"Redline! Redline!"

"Sssss, Ooooo! I'm finna cum, I'm finna cum. Arrrrh!" he moaned out, not caring if he was heard.

"Boy get yo nasty ass up outta me," Amber said angrily, as she shoved Redline off her.

She wiggled her shapely frame back into the confederate grey skintight pants.

"Yo stupid ass act like you don't understand what stop and no means," she said, raising her voice. Amber was more pissed off at breaking her nail fumbling with her belt buckle than she claimed to be at Redline.

"Girl shut your silly ass up before somebody comes in here," Redline snapped, cautiously peeking out of the door. "Fix your mutha fuckin' clothes. You look like you been fucking one of these inmates," he said with a smirk on his face.

"Nigga fuck you! Here, get this shit so I can get the fuck outta here," Amber shoved the cellphone into his hands. She sprayed some Summer Breeze fragrance in the air in front of her, then stepped through the mist.

"Ignorant ass bitch," Redline mumbled, examining the cellphone in his hand.

"Eat my pussy nigga," Amber vexed, as she slapped her ass on the way out the door.

Redline shook his head with a smirk on his face. He looked down at the cellphone in his hand. It was tightly wrapped with black electrical tape that way it couldn't be detected, concealed between the walls of Amber's pussy as she walked through the metal detector. He couldn't resist the temptation that fiddled with his curiosity. The urge to smell the phone played with his mind.

His eyebrows raised up instantly as he sniffed again. To his surprise it didn't stink at all. He grabbed the compressed pound of marijuana and dropped it down one of his pants legs. He removed the tape from the cellphone and rewrapped the tape back on backwards.

That way it would stick to his skin when he cuffed it underneath his nuts. Now making it back to his cellblock without getting caught was the hard part. There were three security gates he had to walk through and at any given moment he could be ordered by any correctional officer to strip out of his clothes, in order to be searched. He inhaled deeply thinking about an old song by ESG.

"Gotta do what I gotta do," Redline mumbled as he walked out of the storage room headed to his cellblock.

$$$

Amber Stacks stood 5'8", 150 pounds of thickness. Her skin complexion was the color of mocha. Her hazel eyes were the most alluring part on her body. She had dimples on both cheeks, and a beauty mole on the left side of her upper lip. Her teeth were whiter than snow, with a smile that made even the hardest criminals melt. Her hair was cut into a short style that resembled Rhianna. Most women spent thousands of dollars trying to counterfeit a perfect figure such as hers.

Amber strutted down the hallway creating a disturbance as usual. Her correctional uniform looked as if it was painted on her body. Her ass swayed with each step she took, and her pussy print stuck out like a sore thumb. Inmates began catcalling and stopping the flow of movement in the hallway.

"Girl you better stop walking like that. You making my tongue on hard," Pharo said, as he licked his lips with sexual thoughts on his mind.

"You looking real nice from the back Miss Stacks," another inmate named YZ yelled out. "You better watch out baby, cause I know magic," he claimed, with a big ass smile on his face.

Amber was feeling herself from the pounding Redline put down on her ass. Plus, the easy $1500 she made for bringing in two cheap ass cellphones, which cost $40 each, and a pound of weed was icing on the cake.

The louder the inmates' cat-called the wetter her pussy became. She was loving the attention this particular day. So instead of threatening them with a disciplinary case like she normally did. She shook her ass a little harder with each step she took. Easy money was her worse addiction. But lately her mind was focused on other things...Redline.

CHAPTER 2

"ENJOYING FREEDOM"
(SOUTHEAST OF THE ASTRODOME)
HOUSTON, TEXAS

Flagg was fresh out the belly of the beast after serving five years flat on a seven-year sentence. He decided it was time to hang up his hustling gloves. Being away from his family and the loss of his mother quickly brought upon the wise decision.

It was a hot sunny Saturday afternoon. His homeboy Peewee was headed over to pick him up so they could turn a few corners. Flagg stared at his reflection in the full-length mirror with a smile on his face. He was looking good, feeling good, and smelling good. He ran a hand over his freshly cut bald fade from Ron, at Ron's Tight Cuts. He was blacker than the ace of spade with two big white diamonds hanging from each earlobe. Many people said he favored the rapper Lil' KeKe. He smoothed out the Earl Campbell jersey and checked his white Levi shorts for any stains. Once he was satisfied, he tilted his baby blue Houston Oilers cap to the left and stepped outside in his patent leather white Jordan's with the North Carolina blue trim. The summer heat attacked Flagg as soon as he opened his front door. He grabbed his cellphone out of his pocket and dialed Peewee's number.

"Where you at man?" Flagg asked aggravated because of the heat.

"I'm outside nigga," Peewee lied, knowing he was just a couple of blocks away.

"Nigga, I ain't got time to play no games. You com—!"

Before he had the chance to finish what he was saying, Peewee turned the corner. Flagg felt the bass in the bottom of his feet as the car came to a stop. The candy paint was still dripping wet, sprayed by Jack's paint and body shop. The sun spilled over the red candy paint dancing off each chrome piece that was visible. The big 225 Buick Electria drop top sitting on a fresh set of vogue-tires, and chrome super pokers, was a slab riders dream. Peanut butter insides, red trimming, wood grain steering wheel, tv screens, fifth wheel bumper kit, chrome grill and woman hood ornament, pop trunk with neon lights displaying WELCOME TO OVERBROOK.

"What's up baby?" Peewee smiled, as the sun toyed with the diamonds in his mouth creating colors as if they were a rainbow.

"Slow motion nigga. Just happy to be free," Flagg stressed, as he got into the car and gave Peewee a firm handshake.

"I see you done came up since I been gone huh," admiring the insides of his car.

"Yea I'm doing a little something. Just trying to stay afloat my nigga," Peewee glanced both directions before he made a left turn.

"What's up, you ready to get this paper like old times?"

"N'all, I'm a try my best to square up this time around pimp. I don't wanna put my family through that madness again," Flagg gazed at Peewee to see if he made himself clear.

"I feel that! But if you ever change your mind, I got cha." Peewee fired up a cigarillo filled with Blue Dream that was sitting in the ashtray.

"Turn that shit up! Flagg said, not trying to entertain the conversation about getting back into the game.

"Damn, what the fuck you got back there?" The bass slammed into his back, it felt like someone was kicking the back of his seat.

"Four eighteen Rocksford Fosgates baby," Peewee bobbed his head as he slowly crossed the railroad tracks on Belfort and Mykawa.

He lowered the music. "My nigga, I even got me a stash spot in this bitch," Flagg shook his head as Peewee volunteered information that should've been kept to himself.

"Turn on the rear defrost and push in the cigarette lighter. Flagg followed his instructions and instantly the radio slid forward transforming and exposing his no longer secret stash spot.

"Man this is a live ass spot. But you know where you fucked up at?" Flagg questioned, looking upside Peewee's head.

"I don't know what you're talking about," Peewee responded confused, glancing in his rearview mirror before he passed the cigarillo.

Flagg knew Peewee had a lot to learn about the game. Making money was the easy part. Now when it came down to keeping the haters out of your business, that was a different story. Whether Peewee wanted to accept it or not, he had a lot of jealous nigga's wishing they could be in his shoes. And when nigga's get to looking and wishing, plots and schemes get to brewing.

"First off, you had someone else hook up your spot. And ain't no telling who else helped 'em out. Then you told and showed me how to get into it," Flagg explained, as he took a deep hit of the Blue Dream.

"You right. But I'm not worried about you my nigga," he glanced in the right-side mirror and merged over in the next lane.

"That's where you fucked up again. Your enemies ain't the niggas you need to watch out for," Flagg took another hit before passing the cigarillo back.

"Your so-called homeboys are the ones you need to worry about," on that note he reached over and turned the music back up.

The potent weed and loud music had each of them in their own zone. They rolled down Belfort at a snail's pace causing traffic. Cars honked and people gave them dirty looks as they zipped by. Flagg gazed out the window and thought about how the hood changed over the years he was away. Peewee had his mind on the knowledge he was absorbing from Flagg.

They came to a stop at a red light on Martin Luther King and Belfort. The music was banging so loud, kids at the bus stop started dancing. Flagg noticed a dude who looked familiar standing at the corner. The dude had on dirty clothes and a beat-up ass Oakland Raiders cap. In his hands he held some newspapers and a spray bottle. The question of where he knew this dude from, bounced around his mind. The dude approached Peewee's car and Flagg quickly noticed the brand-new pair of Air Jordans he had on. It wasn't the fact that they were new, but they haven't even hit the stores yet.

"Get yo dope fiend ass away from my ride," Peewee yelled out as the dude attempted to wipe his windows.

"Bitch ass nigga, you can't hear," he pressed down on the horn.

The dude smiled. That's when Flagg knew something wasn't right. The platinum and diamonds in his mouth didn't add up to his dope fiend disguise.

"Watch o—!"

BOOM! The driver side window exploded along with half of Peewee's head. Blood and brain fragments slapped him in the face. Pieces of Peewee's scalp landed in his lap. Flagg opened the door to escape.

BOOM! Another shot rang out and slammed into his back. The force from the impact propelled him face forward into the concrete. His skull cracked upon contact. Flagg laid in the street trying to maintain consciousness. He stared at the pair of brand-new Air Jordans from underneath the car. But this time he saw the numbers 254 on the side. Someone pulled Peewee's body out of the car and dropped him in the street. That was the last thing he saw before he passed out.

$$$

CHAPTER 3

"SNORTING POWDER, SMOKING SHERMS"
(WAREHOUSE)
KILLEEN, TEXAS

The entire warehouse smelled and felt like a morgue...COLD! The pungent smell of formaldehyde floated throughout the air like an early morning fog. Ralo stood overlooking the crew smoking his second sherm within less than ten minutes. Standing at an even 6 foot, weighing 200 pounds, he felt he was superior over everyone. However, his associates felt differently than the mind-altering drug that was quickly deteriorating his brain. Ralo looked in the direction of the car he drove back from Houston. He couldn't believe he made it back to Killeen without getting pulled over by any State Troopers. Blood and fleshly particles were scattered across the dashboard, front windshield, and the entire passenger side of the car.

"I don't know why you brought that hot ass car back to the spot. That was some dumb ass shit," Tron said, as he played NBA 2K on the 72" flat screen.

"Nigga, how in the fuck you gonna tell me what to bring in my shit," Ralo barked, as spit flew out of his mouth. "You don't pay a mutha fuckin thing around this bitch," him and Tron didn't see eye to eye most of the time.

"It don't matter who's paying for this raggedy mutha fucka. If the laws run up in this bitch we all going to jail," Tron voiced, then drained a three pointer with James Harden, putting the Rockets up by 10 over the Golden State Warriors.

"I don't give a fuck about the laws nigga. You need to be like Fast Blacc and Lil' Brandon. You see how those niggas getting straight to the point breaking that car down," Ralo pointed over in their direction.

"Just like I put one straight in that bitch nigga head. Him and his hoe ass homeboy," Ralo bragged.

He looked at the car again and peeped all the blood. He knew Tron was right, but he hated how Tron always put him on front street in front of the clique.

Fast Blacc and Lil' Brandon were stripping the car of everything that could be sold. Lil' Brandon was in the trunk disconnecting the music. Fast Blacc peeped in the back at Lil' Brandon. Then he gazed over at Tron sitting on the couch playing the game. Ralo stood smoking a cigarette as he mugged Tron upside his head. Fast Blacc turned the key in the ignition forward. He took a quick glance at Lil' Brandon again before he hit the rear defrost button and pushed in the cigarette lighter. As if magic, the stash spot appeared. Fast Blacc wasted no time relieving the box of its contents. He stuffed three stacks of hundreds, a solid gold piece and chain, and a nickel plated .45 into a small duffle bag.

"Fast Blacc!" Ralo yelled out.

"What's up?" he answered, with a nervous look on his face, as his heart rate hammered in his chest.

"Y'all niggas ain't find nothing in that car?" Ralo wondered, texting the dude he was going to sell the rims and music to.

"N'all ain't shit in here," he lied, with a smirk on his face.

"Y'all niggas need to hurry up and put those dummy tires on, so we can get that bitch up outta here,'" Ralo said glancing at Tron, then at the front door as it opened up.

"Guess who's back in the mutha fuckin hooouse, with a fat dick in yo mouth," Bug sang out, as he stepped through the front door.

He dapped Ralo up and walked over to show his cousin Tron some love.

"Maaan! Who brought that bloody mutha fucka in here?" Bug asked, looking the car over with raised eyebrows.

When nobody responded he already knew the answer. He sat down on the couch and dipped a Newport short into a half abstract bottle of water. He wiggled the filter out of the end of the cigarette with his teeth.

"You trying to gamble on this game nigga," Tron asked handing him a cigarette lighter.

"Do a bear shit in the woods," Bug reached for the lighter and blazed up the sherm. POOF! He blew the blaze out and inhaled sharply.

"Bet a hundred on halftime and a hundred on the final," Tron capped, dumping an eight ball on the table then making several lines.

"You can't out cap the captain kinfolk. Bet that and up it a hundred,'" Bug capped back, as the sherm smoke creeped from his lungs and sneaked out of his mouth.

"'Ralo, you want some of this too nigga," he looked back at Ralo who had a vindictive look etched on his face.

"I'm good lil' homie," Ralo darted his eyes at Tron and sucked his teeth.

Ralo felt he could have easily handled Tron, but Bug was a different story. He actually lived by the gun; no questions asked. And going to war against both of them would be foolish on his part.

"Let me hit that shit nigga," Fast Blacc walked up, after discreetly making the duffle bag filled with goodies disappear. He reached for the rolled up $100 bill Tron handed him and snorted a line into each nostril. The pure uncut cocaine shot through his body and made him shiver.

"Damn, where you get this shit from?" Fast Blacc asked, as the white girl drained down the back of his throat.

"If I tell you I gotta kill you," Tron said, as they all laughed.

He passed the sherm to Fast Blacc. Even though he laughed, Tron was dead serious. He didn't like Fast Blacc. It was just something about the way he was always looking around.

Ralo and Lil' Brandon went to dispose of the life sentence on wheels. Bug peeped the tension between Ralo and Tron. He liked Ralo, but blood was thicker than bullshit in his book.

Tron on the other hand stayed one step ahead of the rest. This was a game to the finish. So, it didn't matter who started off winning the race. It was all about the last man who crossed the finish line.

Fast Blacc was in a lane of his own. Whatever doors opened with an opportunity; you best believe he was walking through it. And if anyone was standing in his way blocking the path, violence was the next step.

CHAPTER 4

"LET ME FIND OUT"
(BEN TAUB HOSPITAL)
HOUSTON, TEXAS

Hollywood stood amidst the dead bodies located in the basement of the hospital morgue. Goosebumps involuntarily flooded her skin as she nervously waited on the coroner. She knew it was inevitable before she received a phone call such as this. She was listed as an emergency contact prior to this visit when Peewee was shot the first time.

First their father died in an eighteen-wheeler accident while their mother was seven months pregnant. And a couple of months after that, their mother passed away giving birth to two beautiful twins. Her and Peewee. Hollywood was the oldest by a matter of seconds. They were raised by their grandmother. But ever since she could remember, Hollywood was the one who took care of Peewee.

The medical examiner approached her with a sympathetic look engraved on his face.

"Are you ready miss?" he asked as he gazed with concern.

"I guess so," Hollywood responded blowing air out of her mouth.

"Are you sure?" he walked around the table a cold stiff body laid on.

Hollywood nodded her head up and down even though she wasn't ready to see her brother's dead body. Before she had a chance to change her mind, the coroner drew back the white sheet that concealed the body.

"Nooooo!" she hollered out, before she fainted instantly melting to the floor.

$$$

Flagg lay up in ICU recovering from a gunshot wound to the left shoulder blade and a fractured cranium. The bullet exited his chest mowing down several arteries slightly missing his heart. His head crashing into the concrete caused the most life-threatening damage. There was severe swelling to his brain, and he was stuck in a coma. Tubes ran deep inside his nostrils, mouth, penis, and his lungs draining the fluid. The KGB monitor registered and recorded his vitals. His head was enclosed in a hard-white plastic cast, and his neck was stabilized with a brace.

A petite light-complected nurse checked the monitors and made sure everything was in proper order. She opened the curtain to reveal the beauty of the morning sun. After she made sure her patient was well taken care of, she continued with her normal routine.

As Flagg was stuck in an unconscious state, different episodes of his life projected in his mind. He pictured his two daughters from birth up to recent age. Him and his wife getting married. His release from prison. Him kneeling down beside his mom's tombstone. The dude with the spray bottle and newspapers in his hands. The diamonds sparkling in his mouth. The big chrome Desert Eagle erupting like a cannon. Peewee's blood and brains in his lap. Himself getting shot and forced forward headfirst down to the street top. The numbers 254 on the back of a pair of white shoes...254.

$$$

Hollywood batted her eyelids as she shook her head repeatedly. It took her a good minute until her mind registered. Her hands roamed over her body immediately. She raised up from the couch she was laying on.

"Are you ok?" The medical examiner asked, startling her. Hollywood looked around until she located where the voice was coming from.

"Yes I'm ok," she answered coming to full realization of where she was at.

"There's a bottle of water on the table right next to you," he pointed with the pen he had in his hand. "That was my main concern when I asked you if you were actually ready. I've been through this same scenario numerous times. Whenever you feel like you're ready to leave, you can show yourself out. Have a nice day ma'am," the coroner explained, then disappeared from the room.

Hollywood ran a hand across her face then grabbed the bottle of water. She opened it and took a sip. The vivid image of her brother's half blown off head poked at her thoughts. Question after question tumbled across her mind. Who done it? Why Peewee? Where did it happen? How did they know him? What did they want? She made a vow to herself to find out each and every answer.

Hollywood went to visit Flagg since he was at the same hospital. The woman who called and informed her that Peewee was deceased, also told her someone else was shot with him. Once she heard the name Wilber Hunter, she knew who it was.

The receptionist stated she had to wait in the waiting area until his information was updated into the computer since he was just let out of surgery. Hollywood went to the waiting area with vindictive thoughts cruising around her mind. The words LET-ME-FIND-OUT echoed in her mind. The waiting area was filled to capacity. She got lucky when a man seated next to her got up and left. People stood everywhere there was standing space, and every seat was occupied. Kids were running around hollering, crawling, rolling all over the floor, while their parents either stood or sat lost in their own problems.

"SOMEBODY HELP ME! SOMEBODY HELP ME PLEASE!" a woman screamed out, as she stumbled in through the emergency entrance supporting a man whose clothes were drenched in blood.

The man had his left arm draped over the woman's shoulders, clutching his right side as blood seeped between his fingers. Blood snailed down his face from the two-inch gash across his forehead.

There was a crimson trail left behind marking their path on the white linoleum floor.

"Daaam!" Hollywood mumbled lowly, as her face involuntarily cringed from the amount of blood. After a couple more horrific episodes, Hollywood changed her mind about visiting Flagg. She had seen enough bloodshed for one day, mainly her brothers. She decided to come back another day and visit him. She grabbed her purse and headed for the exit door.

Once outside, the Texas heat attacked the goosebumps that flooded her body from the hospital's cold temperature. She rubbed her hands up and down both arms. Hollywood looked up at the sky and said a silent prayer for her brother Peewee. Redline crossed her mind many times. She really needed him right now. She hopped in her SUV and picked up her phone. She hit track 6 on ALL EYES ON ME by Tupac. "I WON'T DENY IT, I'MA STRAIGHT RIDAH. YOU DON'T WANNA FUCK WITH ME," Tupac barked out of each and every speaker as she drove off.

$$$

CHAPTER 5

"CONCRETE HELL HOLE"
(GLASS HOUSE)

Redline had been in, and out of institutions for over half of his life. Prison wasn't nothing new to him, it was like his home away from home. He was so addicted to making money and hustling, even being locked up didn't stop him.

The main thought on Redlines mind was making it back to his cell-block without getting caught. His heart hammered each step he took down the hallway. Inmates were hollering back and forth to each other across the hallway. Officer's yelled for them to hold the noise down and shut the fuck up. The sound of steel bars slamming shut echoed down the long hallway.

Redline watched as an inmate tried to sneak behind a guard's back to avoid from getting searched. The inmate made it through the gate without the guard seeing him. Before he had a chance to feel like he got away.

A different guard hollered out, "COME HERE!" The inmate ran down the hallway with four guards right on his ass. Redline used the distraction to his advantage. He started walking to the next check gate.

"FUCK!" he mumbled' as he watched Tiger Woods searching inmates as they walked through the gate. Several more guards who were fat and out of shape, finally ran by responding to the disturbance call announced over their walkie-talkies.

Tiger Woods was a robocop guard who made inmates strip out of their clothes at any given moment. Redline had his mind made up, he wasn't taking off his clothes no matter what.

"Hey Tiger Woods! What's up lil' momma," Redline said catching him off guard.

"I got your lil' momma right here bitch!" Tiger Woods snapped back, as he grabbed his crotch area and poked his chest out.

"That's not what that white hoe told me," Redline laughed, as he increased his stride toward his cellblock.

"Don't talk about my wife bitch. Don't talk about my wife," he repeated, turning beet red in the face.

"I'll holla at you later lil' momma," Redline said, as he blew him a kiss and headed through the gate to his cellblock. An old song popped up in his head by D.E.A (Dead End Alliance). "Heart of a Hustla, mind of a G, playa hating niggas can't fuck with me."

As soon as he walked on the cellblock that he was assigned to, several individuals had their eyes on hard (looking and being nosy). Redline made eye contact with his homeboy Big Ro and mouthed the words, "Come on nigga!"

Big Ro was a member of the notorious Southwest Gorillas who ran the streets on the Southwest side of Houston. Him and a dude named Tiger were the only two members on the unit.

Redline walked upstairs, "N wing two row!" he hollered out down into the rotunda to the officer working the first two floors. The rotunda was a deep space in the middle of six different cellblocks. Each cellblock had four rows, so there were four floors, which two guards worked at all times. Each guard was assigned to open and make sure each cell door was secure every day. Also, to notify the inmates of daily activities.

"All that hollering ain't gonna get me to move any faster," yelled a guard named Miss Ross.

She was a bonafide go-getter from New Orleans. She moved to Texas when Hurricane Katrina hit. She'd been stuck in Texas ever since. She had a little sex appeal about herself, but she was a couple of babies out of shape. Miss Ross had a fat ass and a look that said, "I know this pussy is good.'" Her walk captured attention the way she swayed her ass real slow and seductively.

"Miss Ross, can you please open my cell I just got off work," Redline asked, licking his lips mimicking LL Cool J.

"Boy, that was you up here with all that hollering," Miss Ross eyed Redline and admired his good looks. He was light skin with natural wavy hair. He had a medium build and favored the actor Terrance Howard.

"My bad Miss lady, I was just trying to get in my cell," Redline said, then eyed her camel toe print between her legs.

"Don't worry about it, I got you. Just remember me when I need something with your sexy ass..." Miss Ross said, as she strolled away like a prostitute on Telephone road.

"Close that door when you finish too," she yelled, and looked back over her shoulder with a smile on her face.

"Call me Ice Cube, cause today was a good day," Redline sung to himself as he walked down the tier looking out the window. He shook his head at the site of the twelve-foot chain link fence which displayed shining razor wire. He closed the cell door being careful not to lock it. He poked a small piece of mirror out of the cell bars and saw Big Ro walking down the row.

"What's jumpin' my nigga?" Big Ro asked with a smile on his face.

He was a big youngster. He was twenty-five years old, weighed two hundred and fifty pounds. He stood 6'3" and kept a smile on his face. He was serving time for a murder charge which he was fighting to get over turned.

"Man hold me down while I bag this shit up," Redline said, putting up a sheet to block off his wrong doings.

"I got you my nigga, handle your bidness," Big Ro grabbed the small piece of mirror and looked down the row.

"I got that horn you wanted to. Just shoot me eight dollars (eight hundred). You want something off of this elbow?"

"Do you wanna fuck Miss Ross?" Big Ro asked, and peered down the row.

Redline started laughing. Him and over half of the unit wanted to fuck Miss Ross.

"Fix me a cutie, and I'll shoot you anotha four dollars," Big Ro stressed adjusting the mirror so he could see better.

Redline hooked him up and added an extra ounce in for him watching out. He bagged up a total of 11 ounces. He was going to sell each one on the wire (Western Union) for $300 each. He already had individuals who he did business with. It was nothing but for sure money with him. He made $4,000 and some change within two days. He let his clientele use his cellphone so the funds could get quickly transferred. If anyone had any hustle about their self, they were making money around the prison. There were too many women working. And he felt if a woman was working in an institution there had to be something wrong at home. Because most woman who worked on Coffield gave up their pussy in a heartbeat.

Prison was like Baskin & Robbins, instead of 31 flavors, there was close to 5,000. And out of 5,000 men, at least one could make a woman's pussy wet. Temptation was very tempting at times, especially when it came down to making fast easy money. Redline felt he had the game mapped out, quiet as kept. The only problem he had was jealous hating individuals. They were stopping him from blowing the roof off the penitentiary.

Redline never forgot what his homeboy Flagg told him two months ago right before he went home... "I know it's hard to fuck with a lot of these clowns, but you have to bless their game. You got a lot of snake ass niggas slithering around. So, you gotta keep your grass mowed at all times. That way you can see what you're up against. Hand feed your enemies and keep 'em close to you at all times. And last but not least, watch your yes men and the middlemen. Those are the niggas who'll make enemies for you that you never knew you had. Stay prayed up my nigga, cause your chance is right around the corner. You hear me? Look out my nigga! Redline!"

"I feel you man. I just zoned out a minute," Redline said, as he took in every word his homeboy Flagg stressed.

"It takes a minute for you to fall off your game," Flagg said, a few days before he went home.

Outside the Texas prison activity was in full swing. Inmates were on the recreational yard exercising, playing handball, basketball, and lifting weights. While others stood around talking shit to one another and gossiping about the next man. The temperature was well over 100 degrees, as the Texas dry heat lingered.

Redline was laying on his side in his top bunk while Amber stood on her tip toes sucking his member. She licked the base of his shaft slowly and seductively. She worked her tongue in a circular motion around the head of his penis. She slapped his dick on her tongue over and over before attacking it with a vengeance.

Amber slobbered all over his pole making it sloppy wet. She grabbed ahold of his erection and stroked it with passion as she continued to vacuum the head. She felt his body shiver and knew he was about to erupt. Redline jumped down from the top bunk with his dick looking around. Amber pushed him down on the bottom bunk and snatched off his boxers. She stood directly in front of him and unbuckled her belt and undid her pants. She placed one of her feet between his legs and unbuttoned her shirt. With her index finger and thumb, Amber skillfully unhooked her bra. Her perky 34DD's stared him right in the face.

Redline leaned forward and licked around each areola lightly while his hand toyed between her legs. He flicked his tongue over both nipples forcing her to moan out softly. Amber lowered her leg and turned around facing the wall. She slipped her tight pants down over her 45-inch round bubble butt. She placed both hands flat on the wall and bent over with a deep arch in her back. Redline held his dick steady as she perfectly backed up her tail and lowered it down on his hitch.

He leaned back against the wall and thrusted deeper inside her saturated hot canal. She grinded herself slowly until she adjusted to his thickness. Redline propped himself up on both arms and opened his legs wide. Amber held onto the top bunk with both hands and worked her pussy up and down the length of his dick. He scooted to the edge of the bunk and began jabbing further into her hot pocket.

Feeling herself about to explode, she bounced down on his lap and tightened up her walls. Her cum squirted out all over his dick and oozed down the crack of his ass. Amber reached down and placed her hands flat down on the floor and began crashing her ass in his lap.

Redline matched her rhythm and jack hammered aggressively. She started hollering out loudly as he pounded her pussy.

"Ooooo! I'm cumming! I'm cumming. I'm cumming on your dick! Ahhhh!" she moaned out loudly.

Inmates began yelling out, "FUCK THAT PUSSY! FUCK THAT PUSSY!" over and over while they shook their cell bars like mad men trying to escape. Right when Redline was about to shoot his load deep inside of her pussy.

"Man, get yo ass up nigga. Don't nothing come to sleepers but a dream," Big Ro said, shaking the cell door like the gorilla he was.

Redline looked around like he was lost. He gave Big Ro a look that said more than words.

"Nigga, if I had a gun yo ass would've been dead," he sat up on his bunk and waited for his hard on to go down.

"That's why ain't no guns in here nigga. What's up, you wanna blow one before you go to work?" Big Ro asked, looking down the row.

"Who's working the block?" he wandered and jumped down from the top bunk.

"Miss Washington big titty ass. I'll be back, I'm finna go get the doe rolled," Big Ro explained, then walked up the row.

$$$

Amber sat at home on her brown suede four-piece sectional. Her feet rested on a smoke glass coffee table. On the wall directly in front of her hung a big 64-inch Sony flat screen television, showing the latest episode of "Love and Hip Hop". In her lap rested a glass mirror weed tray. She'd just finished twisting up a berry cigarillo filled with Skunk Berry Kush. She clicked the lever on a miniature torch lighter and blazed up the end of the cigarillo.

She inhaled the irresistible drug and enjoyed the savory on the tip of her tongue. Amber depended on her medication constantly, especially the four, 12-hour days she had to work. The feeling of euphoria kidnaped and intensified her senses. Her mind instantly went into currency making mode. She pulled a couple more times holding the smoke hostage within her lungs. After a few seconds she coughed uncontrollably allowing the smoke to escape. She gazed down at her I phone and noticed; she had two more hours before work. She dragged again on the cigarillo then stubbed it out in the ashtray.

She got up and prepared four pounds of weed that were already compressed. She wrapped each one with duct tape. She also covered two cellphones with black electrical tape. Amber was making over $3,000 a day, every four days. That's not including her paycheck she received every month for $2,500. Everything was going good for her, but there was only one problem...Redline.

She was addicted to his dick. It was like she was hooked on some type of drug. Her mind bounced back to Redline hammering her asshole. That was her first time having anal sex, and she couldn't deny the fact that she liked it. Even though she was telling him to stop, her finger that was rubbing her clit persuaded her mind differently. The more she stressed for him to stop, the harder he punished her rectum. The more she said no the deeper he plunged. That was Amber's first time experiencing an orgasm without a hot tongue, finger, or a hard dick penetrating her pussy.

"Damn, this nigga got my mind so fucked up," she said, shaking her head as she picked up her car keys and headed to work.

$$$

Redline turned on his radio. The sounds of Lil' KeKe poured out of a homemade speaker consisted of cardboard, writing paper, and glue. Lil' KeKe voiced lyrically how to be a G until the day that you die. He started brushing his teeth when his cell door popped open. He poked his spy mirror outside of the bars to see what was going on. Big Ro was walking down the row with a smile on his face. He ducked his head and stepped into the cell.

"You got a light nigga?" Big Ro asked, picking up the spy mirror looking down the row. "Then again, I don't even know why I asked yo dopefiend ass that."

Redline laughed, spitting toothpaste all over the sink and wall. He rinsed out his mouth and cleaned up his mess. A cigarette lighter was easy to get, but even easier to get caught with. Therefore, he stuck to the script. He grabbed a pencil that was broken in half. Then he forced a loose razor blade between the lead in order to use as a conductor. He inserted the razor blade into one side of the electrical outlet. Next, he placed a coated piece of wire into the other side. Then he twisted up a piece of toilet paper, touched the end of the wire to the tip of the pencil lead, which ignited and blazed up the toilet paper.

"Here you go," Redline said, holding the wick close to the inward sucking vent so the smoke would get pulled away.

"Fire it up nigga, I got the run," Big Ro tossed him a fat joint and went back to looking out.

"This ain't what I sold you," Redline said between hits.

"N'all, I got that from Tiger a couple of days ago. That's the Wedding Cake right there nigga," he glanced in his direction before peering back into the small piece of glass.

"You gonna smoke it all up nigga?" he joked.

"Here," Redline exhaled blowing smoke into the vent. He swapped positions and became the lookout. The Wedding Cake had him in a medicated state. His mind began drifting thinking about Hollywood.

He couldn't wait to talk to her when he went back to work. His home boy Pyrex held his cellphone down. That way he didn't have to worry about any late-night random cell searches from any correctional officers.

"What the fuck are y'all doing?" Miss Carpenter said, snatching the spy mirror out of Redlines hand startling them both.

"Boy, I see your big ass," Big Ro tried to duck off to the side. "Y'all might as well finish smoking that shit. Because I'm writing both of y'all ass up," she threatened, then walked towards the end of the row.

"Man, what the fuck is wrong with you nigga?" Big Ro asked with a meek expression on his face.

"You fell asleep on the job," he smiled shaking his head side to side.

"That good gas had me out there man," he stressed honestly. "What you think she gonna do?"

"Nothing! Miss C the bitch who brought this shit in. Nigga we lucky it was her instead of Miss Reese police ass," Big Ro flushed the doobie down the toilet.

"Y'all gotta stop slipping like that. Y'all know these white folks don't play," Miss Carpenter voiced, then threw the spy mirror on the bottom bunk and strutted away. She gazed into each and every cell as she passed by.

"You wanna put anotha one in the wind?" Big Ro asked with raised eyebrows.

"N'all I'm good. I'm finna get ready for work call," he said, eyeing the clock radio.

"They finna drop out any minute," Redline said, shuffling around the cell preparing for work. He rubbed on some knock off Jimmy Choo Man Blue oil he bought from another inmate. He was feeling good, smelling good, and looking good.

"Nigga you putting on smell good like you finna go to the club or something," Big Ro capped, as he sniffed in the good smelling fragrance.

"Nigga, you know this shit smells good," Redline sat on the toilet and bent down to put on his shoes.

"You know I never been a hater. Let me use some of that shit," Big Ro smiled, reaching for the oil.

"SIX O'CLOCK WORK CALL FALL OUT TO ONE ROW. SIX O'CLOCK WORK CALL FALL OUT TO ONE ROW!" an officer repeated over the loudspeaker.

Redline disguised all of his minor contraband in different spots within the cell. Bi Ro stood in front of the cell door mean mugging whoever peeked his way. The cell doors opened simultaneously.

Big Ro was the first one out of the cells. He divided the crowd of inmates like Moses parted the red sea. Redline followed suit right behind him. And if looks could actually kill, both of them would've been dead as two frogs trying to hop across Interstate 10. They both made eye contact with Tiger who was sitting on the back bench up against the wall with a towel around his neck.

After Miss Carpenter secured all of the cell doors on one and two rows, she opened up the dayroom door to allow all inmates access. Redline and Big Ro made their way to the back where Tiger sat alone.

"What's up Redbone?" Tiger joked, with a smile on his face advertising the numerous diamonds in his mouth.

"You need to ask yo baby daddy, big as yo stomach is," Redline jabbed back, making his way between him and the bench. He rubbed on Tiger's fat pot belly before sitting down in the middle of him and Big Ro.

"See if your girl wanna move ten cans. If not, just bring me an elbow," Tiger voiced, mentally calculating his profit redundantly. "Here goes a thee for whatever jumps off,'" he inconspicuously passed Redline ten $100 dollar bills, neatly folded, tied inside of a latex glove finger.

"I want ten packs off the cans. You know we already understood on the bows," Redline responded, discreetly making the thumb size pack disappear into a secret pocket sewed in the middle of his shorts.

"Tell Miss Stacks fine ass I got a c-note for some of that pussy," Big Ro smirked, resting his huge long arms on the back of the bench. They all started laughing.

The dayroom was intended for recreational purposes. There were two 36" televisions located high on the brick wall resting on steel shelves. One television stayed on ESPN, or some type of sports program all day. The other one was for any type of program the inmates agreed upon. Three rows of benches stretched across the middle of the dayroom. Each row held about 16 to 20 inmates. Two big industrial fans were perched on the walls higher than the TVs.

Posted up in the back of the dayroom was only a urinal and a sink. Therefore, if an inmate had to take a dump, he was shit out of luck. He had to wait until the correctional officer's allowed all inmates to go in their cells, which was usually every hour. And for the unfortunate ones who couldn't hold their mud, they had to find something to take a shit in and throw it out the window.

Bolted and welded into the concrete floor were three square cement and steel tables. Each table had four steel circle seats, were inmates sat and wrote letters to their families. While a majority of the inmates occupied the tables to gamble on chess and dominoes.

"Fuck! I pass man," Sam pounded on the table from anger.

They were playing a game called Knock.

"Yo stupid ass keep passing me like I got the mutha fuckin down," he said exasperated, sneering at an inmate named PG from Dallas.

"Don't worry about him. I got his ass," YZ voiced, as he slammed down big four. That left him with one domino, which was big six. And if you dominoed with big six, everyone would lose. It was basically a hold and pass your man game.

"Man, shut yo bitch ass up. You been bumping all day nigga. Dooky mouth mutha fucka," Terrell barked, flexing his jaw and curling up his mouth.

"Don't talk to my ho like that. I'm the only one who can check the bitch," PG smiled, rubbing on YZ's hand.

"You got a ugly ass ho," Sam chuckled out loud placing his domino down on the table.

Redline looked over at them playing Knock. He was usually one of the four talking shit and passing time. Today was his first day back to work, and playing dominoes was the last thing on his mind.

"What the fuck you laughing at, snitch ass nigga. Make me slap yo mutha fuckin ass," YZ snapped, taking his anger out on Terrell.

"Nigga you slap me, the life flight gonna land on the rec yard," Terrell stressed, pointing his index finger towards the recreational yard.

Everyone at the table started laughing, including a few other inmates that were standing around watching the game.

"POOOW!" YZ stood over Terrell with his palm still open. Blood dripped off of Terrell's lip from the fierce pimp slap.

"I told you I know magic nigga. See how you turned into a ho," YZ raised his voice for everyone to hear.

Redline had just made it out the door for work call when the incident occurred. But he heard and witnessed the slap up close in person. He peeped Terrell on the floor digging his hand inside of his knee brace.

"Work call fall out!" the turnkey ordered. Redline hurried off the cellblock and headed to work.

YZ stood talking shit like a world class comedian. Not aware of death within a couple of feet away from him.

"Didn't I tell y'all this nigga got that pussy," he carried on blindly to his surroundings.

Terrell sprung up on his feet with the promptness of a jaguar and pounced on his prey. In his right hand he held a three-inch rod sharpened to perfection at the tip.

"Bitch-ass-nigga!" he emphasized each time he pierced the spiked tip into his neck.

"I-told-yo!" Terrell impaled the shank striking his jugular vein causing blood to pulsate in a mist.

YZ slowly dropped down to the floor. He crawled underneath the table and died in a puddle of his own blood. He'd always stressed daily, that if he died bury him under the Knock table. His wish finally came true.

$$$

CHAPTER 6

"RIDING HIGH"
(FIFTH WARD)
HOUSTON, TEXAS

F ast Blacc crept down Lockwood with no respect for the law or
anyone else on the road. The trunk on his car rattled so loud,
it sounded like it was about to fall off. The bass pounded the
concrete with no regret. The bass was banging with such force, each
time he flicked the cigarette lighter to life it blew out. His anticipation
for the mind-altering drug, and the taste of the formaldehyde on the
tip of his tongue was enough pressure. He turned down the music and
lit the sherm. POOF! He quickly blew out the blue flame then inhaled.
Within three strong drags, the sherm was history. A crooked smile
snailed across his face as the powerful drug took effect. His vision
became crystal clear and his hearing was sharper than ever.

An old couple drove their car along the side of his 1988 candy blue
drop top Seville. A white woman with a head of grey hair stared at him
from the passenger's side window. Fast Blacc turned the music back up
and startled the old woman. She gave him a disgusting look. He shot
the middle finger at her and cranked up his system even louder. The
old man driving the car accelerated and passed him up.

A big chrome .45 automatic sat in his lap as he gripped the wood
grain steering wheel with his left hand. Fast Blacc bobbed his head as
he rested his elbow on the armrest with his cellphone in his hand. He
peered at the vibrating rearview mirror and peeped red and blue

flashing lights. He sat his phone down and reached for the .45 automatic. His gaze shot back to the rearview mirror.

His heartrate increased the closer the police car came. His right index finger fondled the trigger aggressively with blood on his mind. Going back to prison was not an option. His thumb hit the safety as he pulled into the sandwich shop on the corner of Lockwood and Stone Wall. To his surprise the police car darted right by him running the red light crossing the bridge over Interstate 10. He clicked the safety back on and wiped the beads of sweat off his face with his forearm.

People inside of the sandwich shop shot daggers with their eyes due to the loud bass making the windows shake. Mumbling obscene words to himself, he lowered the music. He reached for his cellphone to make a call. The line rang twice before someone answered.

"What's up dark chocolate," Tiffany answered with a cheerful attitude.

"Coolin', you busy?" Fast Blacc asked, scoping his surroundings.

"N'all I just got through cleaning up, why?" she responded, answering a question with a question.

"Just wanted to know could I swing through?" Fast Blacc noticed a woman and her two kids walking out of the sandwich shop. The nosey woman gawked inside of his car. Her eyes bulged once she saw the huge, shiny, chrome gun on his lap. She grabbed her kids and rushed away to her car.

"Yea come on. Where are you at now?" Tiffany wondered, mainly to see how much time she had to get herself together.

"Down the street on Lockwood," he said, unscrewing the cap on the brown vanilla extract bottle. It was filled with the mind-boggling drug.

"Ok, I'll be here," Tiffany said before ending the call.

Fast Blacc patrolled his surroundings again and gazed at each mirror. He bit down on the filter of the cigarette and removed it. He baptized the tip of the Newport short into the piss colored substance then screwed the top back on. Next, he inhaled sharply twice causing the liquid to coat the entire cigarette. He lit the cigarette and watched the fire burn on the end like a candle. He blew it out and took a slow deep drag. The drug took charge immediately. He placed his car into gear and glanced both ways before easing off into traffic. Several drivers blew their car horns with pure aggravation.

Fast Blacc drove his slab in front of 5 o'clock traffic at a crawling pace with his sound system blasting. He popped open his trunk and expressed how he really felt. Flaunting brightly were the words "THE HOOD I DIE FOE!" with a hand displaying the fifth ward sign. He took his last hit off the sherm and made a left turn on Brackenridge Street.

Tiffany lived in a small three-bedroom house by herself. She was 22 years old with no kids. She attended Texas Southern University majoring in Medical Technology. She was trying her best to get out of the hood. However, the magnetic force refused to let her go. Tiffany stayed in the third house on the right. He lowered his music before turning into her driveway. He didn't bother calling because he felt she heard the music when he turned on her block.

Fast Blacc watched as she stepped outside. The summer breeze blew the leaves in her front yard. Tiffany turned around to lock her door. Her ass cheeks chewed up her shorts on the right side. He licked his lips and rubbed his crotch area. She turned around and walked towards the car. Her hair was in a neat freshly done ponytail that stopped in the middle of her back. Her skin complexion was the color of bronze. She sported a small black t-shirt that read fifth ward's finest in white letters. The white skintight shorts left little to the imagination. The print of her labial was boldly visible. Her legs were oiled to perfection. Many people said she resembled the singer Sade but only darker. She opened the front door and slid in the passenger's seat.

"What's up black boy?" she said before the door even closed.

"Yo fine ass riding this dick," he smirked, as he rubbed softly up her thigh.

"We got all day for that. First, we gotta go get this money. I know this trick who's sitting on a nice piece of change you down?" Tiffany explained, moving his hand between her legs.

"Bitch, don't try to play a pimp hoe! You already know I'm all about that paper," Fast Blacc snapped, trying his best to ignore the moist heat coming from between her legs.

"Ok Daddy! Let's go get this paper," she moved his hand from between her legs and buckled up her seat belt.

"Go towards Lockwood and make a right. When you get to Lorrain make another right. Then turn right on Calvacade, and make a left on the first street," Tiffany explained, as they backed out of her driveway.

Fast Blacc fired up a Newport as his mind played over his daily events up until now. He wasn't worried about Tiffany setting him up or trying to play him like a chump. He used all his women to his benefit. And if they weren't helping him in any form or fashion, their number would've been deleted out of his contacts. The lick Tiffany had played with his brain. He wanted to know more information.

"What kind of play you got?" Fast Blacc wondered, as he glanced in her direction. He made a right turn on Calvacade and raised up the convertible top.

"It's this trick named Low Low I know. He hustles out of a house on the next block," she explained.

"Make a left right here," she pointed excitedly.

"All you have to do is break into the trunk of his car and get the stash. Pull over in front of that vacant house," she nodded in the direction with her head.

"He stays across the street. The house with the old blue car in the yard," she said, checking herself out in the sun visor mirror.

She applied a light coat of lip gloss on her pouty lips. Fast Blacc looked over the scene a few times for anything suspicious, or any nosey ass neighbors. He had to give it to Tiffany. The set up was quiet, nobody outside, and inconspicuous.

"I'll call your phone when it's time to move. Do you know how to get into the trunk?" Tiffanny asked, getting out of the car slowly with an arch in her back.

"You let me worry about that momma. Just hit me when you're ready," he stressed, grabbing a Texans cap from off the backseat. He put the cap on his head and pulled it down over his eyebrows.

"Ok Daddy!" she closed the door carefully, not to make any loud noises.

She walked across the street with her shorts crawling up her ass. And if anyone was looking, they weren't paying him any attention. Fast

Blacc used Tiffany's fat ass jiggling as a quick distraction. He popped open his trunk, jumped out, grabbed a flat head screwdriver, and was back in the car before her fine ass reached the front door. He watched as she knocked on the front door.

$$$

Low Low was well known around the nickel (FIFTH WARD). He'd been in the game for well over 20 years. Everywhere you went on the northside Low Low's name was mentioned. He sold a little bit of everything. And every drug his hands came across was of good quality. Ever since he beat his last drug charge, he kept his hustling to a minimum. His name was ringing too much on the streets, and too many people knew him.

But nobody knew him better than Tiffany Johnson. Low Low opened the front door before she even finished knocking.

"Damn boy, you must've been peekin' out the damn window," she joked, brushing her ass up against him as she stepped inside.

"Girl, you know I'm crazy about your fine ass," he smiled, rubbing a hand over his fat stomach. Low Low stood 5'11", weighed 330 pounds. He was built and had corn row braids like number 99 who played for Tampa Bay Buccaneers.

"I know what yo ass crazy about," she teased, poking him in the stomach like the Pillsbury Dough Boy. Low Low smiled and turned on some music. Tiffany turned around and swayed her coke bottle figure to the sexy crooning sound of Luther Vandross.

He sat down on the soft white leather couch and enjoyed the view. She bent all the way over and looked back. She pulled her shorts to the side and revealed her pretty, plump, bald, pussy. She inserted two fingers in and out of her honey cave in a rapid motion. Low Low had his dick in his hands pumping away. He cummed in his t-shirt he had on. Tiffany jabbed her fingers into her coochie faster and faster. The smacking sound traveled throughout the house.

"You ready girl? I can't take it no more," Low Low got up and went into the bedroom.

"Freaky mutha fucka!" she mumbled, sucking her juices off her fingers.

$$$

Fast Blacc sat in the car wondering what the fuck was taking her so long. He smoked on his eighth cigarette. After his fourth one, he was contemplating on leaving her. Jealous thoughts of her pleasing another nigga played with his mind. Plus, his other bitch Mona kept blowing up his phone. He kept sending her straight to voice mail, because he already knew what she wanted. He gazed down at his platinum Cartier wrist wear. He was going to give her 10 more minutes. Then he was burning off with, or without her ass.

$$$

Tiffany walked into the bedroom and saw Low Low face down ass up. He had a 10 inch strap on, and a bottle of baby oil at the end of the bed. She shook her head and strapped on the rubber dildo. She wore a smile on her face as she grabbed the baby oil and squeezed it in his asshole. She thought about how Fast Blacc punished her pussy the last time they had sex.

Tiffany's eyes widen at the thickness and length of the stiff rubber dick. She pushed the head of it in slowly. Low Low's butthole welcomed the massiveness with genuine hospitality. He backed his ass up like a real pro. Tiffany went to work. She slammed in and out of his rectum like she was a porno star. Low Low met each thrust and spread his butt begging for more. Tiffany had sweat dripping down her face.

"Take this dick bitch! Take this dick!" she said, pretending to be Fast Blacc when he lays pipe to her.

"Ooooo Yeeea! Work that dick. Faster, faster, faster," Low Low ordered, reversing his ass to meet each pound.

"Aaaah, I'm cu-cu-cu cumming," he gasped out then collapsed flat on the bed with her on top of him.

"FUCK!" Tiffany said exhausted. She quickly took off the strap on. She snatched her $500 off the dresser. "I work hard for my money," she sung an old Donna Summers song. "Low Low. I'm finna go," she walked back over to the bed and looked down at him.

The strap on was still buried deep in his ass. He was out cold with a smile on his face. She snapped a picture of him just in case she needed to black mail him. She texted Fast Blacc...GO!

The incoming text snapped him out of his trance. He hopped out of the car and walked right across the street. Without wasting any time, he pulled the screwdriver out and went to work on the lock. The car was an old Cadillac with the batwing tail lights. It took him less than a minute to break the lock.

He opened the trunk, "What the fuck?" he wondered out loud.

The inside of the trunk was completely empty. Anger flooded over his entire body. He turned around to leave, but his intuition tapped him on his shoulder. He reached into the trunk and pulled up the carpeted cardboard bottom. A smile Nascar-ed across his face. Fast Blacc grabbed the backpack and hightailed back to his vehicle.

Once inside of his car he looked around. Satisfied the scene was still looking the same, he unzipped the backpack. His eyes lit up with greed. Inside was rolls of money wrapped with rubber bands. He snatched out five rolls and stuffed them underneath his seat. He zipped the bag up and texted Tiffany. She came outside instantly.

She hopped in the car and closed the door. "We good?" she asked, blowing air down the front of her shirt.

"Yea, it's all in the backpack," he said as he drove away.

"It took yo ass long enuff," he sneered, looking over her appearance.

"He must've put that dick on you real good the way you sweating," he sparked up another cigarette.

"Boy whatever! How much money we got?" she asked opening up the backpack.

"Oooo, today was the day," Tiffany smiled when she saw all the rolls of money.

She laced Fast Blacc up on what went down between her and Low Low. Once he found out, the real, he couldn't believe it. He loss all respect for Low Low, who was known around the hood as a standup individual. He glanced at Tiffany then nodded his head with a grin on his face.

They made it baek to her house. Tiffany counted and divided the loot. She counted out $25,000, $12,500 each. Plus, the $500 she made for pleasing Low Low. She was $13,000 to the good. She knew Fast Blacc cuffed $5,000 of the money. Her and Low Low counted and made 30 rolls. Each roll consisted of $1,000 dollars. Now she knew he couldn't be fully trusted.

Fast Blacc stuffed 6 rolls into each front pocket and left the $500 on the table. He slapped Tiffany on the ass for her job well done. Now he had another dilemma to deal with...Mona.

$$$

CHAPTER 7

"BELLY OF THE BEAST"
(GLASS HOUSE)

Redline just made it to the other side of the unit when numerous correctional officer's darted by him from every direction. Their walkie talkies crackled noisily down the hallway. His eyes widen and his neck swiveled back and forth. His adrenaline kicked in causing his heartbeat to quickly accelerate. He quickened his pace towards the Administrative Segregation cellblocks. Redline was greeted by a warning sign above the security gate. CAUTION YOU ARE ENTERING HIGH SECURITY AREA. ALL INMATES ARE SUBJECT TO BE STRIP SEARCHED UPON ENTERING AND LEAVING THIS AREA.

He was oblivious to the killing that occurred on the cellblock he was assigned to. However, he didn't think twice about seizing the opportunity of not getting strip searched. Because anytime chaos erupted around the unit, it was a free pass for hustlers to move contraband and get paid.

Not one correctional officer was in the hallway. Redline rushed to the cellblock he cleaned up every day. His job description consisted of sweeping, mopping floors, passing out food trays. He was a janitor working for free, with great paying benefits.

The cellblock he was assigned to clean was housed with gang related inmates. The first two rows were occupied by Ayran Brother Hoods, better known as AB's. The second two rows which were located up a set of stairs, were filled with Texas Syndicate (TS) inmates. Redline had gained trust with over half of the cellblock. And for the ones who didn't trust him, they trusted and respected the ones who did. He quickly completed his job tasks with only one thing on his mind...talking to Hollywood.

"What's going on nigger?" Gut said, putting emphasis on the N word.

"Been waiting for you to come back," Gut was the leader of the AB's on his cellblock. And, one of Redline's best clienteles.

"Ain't nothing honky," Redline chuckled, snapping out of his thoughts. "I thought you was sleep. You had your door covered up," he said almost in a whisper.

"Just being on the safe side. You know I stay on this horn damn near all day," Gut smiled, adjusting his Ray Ban eyewear. "I need another pound of that Bobby Brown!" he stressed, trying to mimic a black man's voice and body language.

"You need to stick to being a Klansmans peckerwood!" Redline responded to his racial lame attack.

The money he was making off Gut was really good. So, putting up with his ignorance was tolerated. Also, the $10,000 steel door that separated the two of them.

"You know the ticket. Have the bread there in an hour, and I'll bring it tomorrow," he instructed lowly, gazing up and down the row.

"I'm going to send fifteen hundred. I want thirty-five cans of worm dirt (dipping tobacco)," Gut said arrogantly rubbing his hands together.

"Bet, just make sure the funds are right," he grabbed the push broom and continued sweeping. Redline noticed out of his peripheral someone standing in front of each cell door he passed by. Each racist soldier stood patiently with hostility oozing out of their pores. He knew if Gut would've given the word; he might not had made if off the cellblock alive.

"E wing turnkey!" Redline yelled out to the correctional officer who was opening and closing the doors.

"What do you need?" The turnkey asked, with a frown on his face.

"Need to get a mop bucket off of D wing," he lied, looking the officer straight in the eyes. "I just finished sweeping up, all I have to do is mop," Redline wiped sweat away from his nose with the back of his hand.

"Alright make it fast," the turnkey ordered, opening both doors. "Close these doors when you finish too," he instructed before walking off.

Redline rushed up the stairs taking the steps by threes. He saw the Eye (spy mirror) as soon as he turned the corner. Pyrex always kept his Eye hanging out of the cell door. That way if a correctional officer decided to run down on him; he would see them coming. Redline smiled shaking his head side to side.

"What's up hustla," he said, sticking his index finger in one of the many quarter size holes of a steel plate that covered the entire cell front.

"Same shit different smell," Pyrex calmly said, shaking Redline's finger.

"Say man, your girl been blowing up the horn since you left. I told her I would tell you when I saw you. She sounded like something was wrong," he explained, squinting his eye looking in the spy mirror.

"Good looking out. Let me get that horn so I can go and call her," Redline peeked back at the door looking for the turnkey. Getting caught with a cellphone wasn't on his list of things to do. Pyrex slid the horn underneath the cell door. Redline scooped it up and tucked it underneath his armpit.

"Be careful nigga," Pyrex said with sympathy, as he watched him disappear around the corner.

Redline grabbed the mop bucket, slammed the door shut, and rolled it to the cellblock he was working on. He secured the door behind him and darted up the stairs to two row. When Pyrex told him, Hollywood had been calling back to back; he knew something was wrong. None of Gut's flunkies were standing in their doors when he came back through. And Gut had his cell front blocked off again.

"Lookout Tanner!" Redline said quietly tapping on his cell door.

"What's up cousin?" Tanner asked confused, rubbing the sleep out of his eyes.

"I need you to hold me down. I'm finna go to that world real fast," he uttered.

"Ok cousin," Tanner responded, as he watched Redline go into the empty cell next door to him.

$$$

Hollywood stared at herself in the full-length mirror on her bathroom door with a bleak expression on her face. The hot steamy shower washed a river of tears down the drain. Her reflection was a 5'6", 145-pound work of art. 36DD's, 26-inch waist, with a 46-inch round bottom. Her skin tone was the complexion of a honey roasted almond. Her natural wavy, long black hair reached down to the middle of her back. Big brown doe shaped eyes, button nose, pouty juicy red lips. Her stomach was flat enough to iron clothes on.

Hollywood didn't have any friends. The only person she confided in was in prison awaiting parole...Redline. She rubbed baby oil all over her flawless body, before easing her figure into a matching green and black panty and bra set. She forced a smile on her face then slid into one of Redline's favorite shirts.

Hollywood met Redline in high school at the young age of 16. She had a crush on him and always did his homework. But like most boys, he didn't see the bigger picture. All he saw was a girl who wanted to do his work all the time. And who was he to complain, especially when he didn't do his homework anyways.

She genuinely smiled thinking about their past. That was over 10 years ago. Her cellphone vibrated in a circle. The buzzing sound snapped her out of her daze. She reached for her phone off the countertop and noticed she had 6 missed calls from Redline.

Redline sat in the dark on the stainless-steel toilet and cursed under his breath. He'd called Hollywood several times and still no answer. A frown crept across his face as the muscles in his jaw flexed. He looked down at the phone in his hands and dialed again. The phone rang and his mind wondered...what the hell is going on? The line rang again...why the fuck she ain't answering the phone? Right when the next thought tapped at his brain, she answered.

"Hey baby," Hollywood answered almost in a whisper.

"Are you ok? Pyrex told me you been blowing the phone up trying to reach me," Redline stammered, rubbing a hand over his head.

"Somebody killed Peewee. They shot him in the face and took his car. Flagg got shot too. I been trying to call and tell you what was going on. Baby I really need you right now. You're the only one in my life I can talk to," she explained in one deep hurried breath. Redline was the only person she could truly open up to.

It didn't matter, he was always there to listen and give her positive advice. Hollywood felt that Jehovah was allowing her to suffer because she was a bad person. She didn't know what to expect following the death of her brother Peewee.

"What! Flagg got shot too. What were they doing together?" Redline questioned, in a raised voice forgetting where he was at.

He sat there dumbfoundedly listening to Hollywood explain the death of her brother. Her deep emotional pain was felt over the phone. His mind drifted back to his homeboy Flagg. His brain refused to register the information it was being fed. Flagg was like a brother from another mother to him. A brother he wished for but never had. A brother he was willing to go all out for, whether wrong or right.

"One time two row!" one of the AB's yelled out informing the others. Simultaneously the entire row yelled out, "ONE TIME TWO ROW!"

"Look out cousin the laws are coming," Tanner hollered out to Redline. He called out to Redline a couple more times before he started beating on the wall. Redline was so lost in his thoughts over Flagg getting shot, he barely heard Tanner pounding on the wall right next door to him.

"What's up man?" he asked aggressively with a scowl on his face.

"The fucking laws are coming bro," Tanner voiced, as he peered in his spy mirror watching the correctional officer walk towards his cell.

Redline pulled his pants down and sat back on the toilet like he was taking a dump. He held the cellphone between his legs ready to flush it if necessary. His heartrate sped up. His legs bounced nervously. Redline saw the officers shadow approaching the cell door.

"Boy what the fuck are you doing?" Amber questioned with a smile on her face, knowing she startled him. "You in here jacking off," she said playfully, gazing up the row before stepping into the dimly lit cell.

"Damn bitch, you scared the shit outta me," Redline exhaled, blowing air between his lips. He glanced down at the cellphone.

"I know. I smell your stinky ass," she joked, holding her nose shut.

"You's a lying bitch. What you got for me?" he stood and pulled his pants back up. He made sure again that the cellphone was hung up. He didn't need Hollywood hearing Amber talking about anything off the wall. Cause like himself, Amber spoke her mind freely.

"I got a pound right now, and a few more in the car. Somebody wired fifteen hundred too. I got it thirty minutes ago," she read the information off her iPhone watch.

"Keep that bread. Bring me another elbow and thirty-five cans of dip. I need ten cans of tobacco too," Redline said, while texting Hollywood to let her know that he would call her back later.

"Nigga your ass is short. Where is the rest of my money?" she asked, placing her hands on her hips with both legs spread apart. "Don't give me that puppy dog ass look."

"Be quiet. I got yo mutha fuckin money," he dug into the pocket sewed inside of his shorts. He pulled out the $1,000 Tiger gave him for the tobacco or an elbow. He took out five c-notes and handed them to her.

"What the fuck is this?" Amber sourly asked eyeing the money in her hand. In her palm she held five neatly folded $100 bills the size of a starburst piece of candy.

"That's five hundred, plus the fifteen hundred. You do the math," Redline said, looking directly at her fat monkey print between her legs.

"That's a bet! We good," she said, mimicking Redline's words as she put the money in her pocket. She reached inside of her protective vest and pulled out the compressed elbow. "I'll bring the other one when I go on break. And I'll bring the thirty-five cans of snuff, and ten cans of tobacco tomorrow," she frowned, fanning herself with her hand.

"Just make sure you bring my shit tomorrow. I don't need no excuses bitch," this time he looked her directly in the eyes.

"Nigga suck on this," Amber rubbed the mound between her legs and walked out of the cell. She wanted to feel Redline's pretty lips smack and slurp up her nectar. She felt the wetness between her thick thighs.

Redline waited until Amber left off the cellblock. Once he heard the steel door slam shut; he tucked the cellphone and placed the elbow underneath his armpit before stepping out the of the cell.

"Appreciate that Tanner. I got something for you tomorrow. For real," he said confidently.

"It ain't nothing. I know you screwing Miss Stacks, huh," Tanner wondered, wishing he was fucking her fine black ass.

"N'all cousin we just cool," he lied with a straight face. "Let me go drop this off to Gut, I'll holla at you," Redline walked off and stopped a few cells down. "Lookout Honky! I'll drop off the cans tomorrow," he slid the elbow underneath the cell door and eased away.

Redline called Hollywood again before he took the phone back to Pyrex. Hollywood was emotionally disturbed, and that alone had him feeling remorseful because he wasn't there to be the man that she needed. While he was talking to Hollywood, Redline sensed she wasn't really into the conversation. It was like her mind was somewhere else, because her thinking was illogical.

Redline walked around the cellblock cleaning up each dayroom. He was sweeping up trash, and literally raking in cash. He sold two elbows (pounds of weed) in quarters for $1,000 each. The last pound he sold all zips (ounces) for $300 apiece. Once all the money was transferred and cleared, that was when he made all his drops. Amber made her ends with no complaints. And each and every one of Redline's customers were satisfied.

Four days had passed by quickly and Redline had pulled in over $12,000 with ease. He roamed around the cellblock trying to locate Amber. Today was the last day of her card, and he wanted to talk to her about going to Houston to keep Hollywood company during her time of grief. Amber knew how Redline felt for Hollywood, so she tried her best to keep her feelings in check.

But she couldn't keep her thoughts off of Redline's fat red pole and juicy red lips.

"Hey boss lady! Do you have any work for me to do?" Redline

inquired smartly, eyeing the redneck turnkey that was standing in hearing distance.

"Matter of fact I do. The dayroom on three row needs to be moped. And don't be up there trafficking and trading either, or I'm gonna write your ass up," Amber voiced sternly, pulling out her disciplinary handbook.

"And if you think I'm playing try me," she glanced at the turnkey before allowing Redline to enter the cellblock she was working on.

Redline mumbled underneath his breath. Noticing the turnkey wasn't paying them any mind, she walked up the stairs. Redline was pretending like he was actually sweeping. Amber shook her head and laughed. There wasn't a piece of paper on the floor.

"Boy, you could've at least threw some trash on the floor," she continued to shake her head side to side smiling.

"You know I gotta play my role to the fullest. Say all bullshit aside, I need a big favor," Redline stared at her holding the push broom in his hands. The look he had on his face made Amber change her friendly demeanor.

"I'm not doing that! I told your mutha fuckin ass when I first met you. I'll smuggle shit in, but I'm not helping break nobody out. You got the wrong bitch," she expressed with her eyebrows raised and one hand on her hip.

"Ain't shit funny. I ain't playing with you," she turned to walk away.

"Bitch, ain't nobody trying to escape," he snapped, halting her in her tracks. "I need you to go to the H and check up on my girl. Her brother got killed and she's not herself. I want you to go and kick it with her and keep her company. I wired over twelve racks to you," That made her quickly about face.

"Just give Hollywood nine racks and keep the rest. Is that cool with you?'" Redline asked gazing in her hazel eyes, waiting for her to say yes.

"You already know I'ma say yes. So, you can take that dumb and dummer look off your face," she reached into her shirt pocket and pulled out a small notebook pad and pen. "Give me her number so I can call her when I get there."

"I told her you were coming down to bring her some money. She already knows that you're cool people," he explained before giving her the number. "Make sure my girl is alright Amber. You hear me? She's all I got."

"Boy I got you. Let me get back downstairs before that pecker-wood comes up here. I'll catch a flight out there tomorrow morning. Stay out of trouble Adrain Jones," she called him by his government name before walking downstairs.

Redline continued his cleaning routine throughout the night. Amber made her last drop a little after 2 o'clock in the morning. So, before the 6 o'clock day shift checked in, everybody who wired Redline funds, was satisfied and well taken care of. Hollywood was no longer a stressful situation for him, thanks to Amber. He could rest without having to worry about her being alone during her grieving stages of losing her brother.

His homeboy Flagg weighed down on his mind heavily. However, all he could do was pray to Jehovah about it. His parole date was slowly creeping up. And his parole lawyer Lori Redman said he had a good chance at making his next parole. With freedom racing through his mind, Redline turned in his cleaning equipment and went to take a hot shower. The next four days he was off, so therefore he would have to wait to check up on Hollywood and Amber. And when a certain thing is toying with your thoughts, four days can seem like an eternity.

$$$

CHAPTER 8

"HOMICIDAL MANIAC"
(ARMY BASE)
FORT HOOD, TEXAS

Ralo rolled around shermed out in a black-on-black stolen Yukon Denali. The owner of the SUV was lying dead inside of a McDonald's dumpster. The body had not yet begun to smell, but it was discovered. Flies investigated the scene lured by the scent of dried up blood and stinky trash.

Ralo stole the SUV less than 24 hours ago. He snatched the military identification card that was hanging from the rearview mirror. He didn't look anything like the young recruit. The only thing they favored was the exact same skin color. He studied the information trying his best to remember the birthdate if needed. The name Desmond Ford was easy to remember.

Ralo lowered the music as soon as he turned onto military property. Bushwick Bill whispered homicidal thoughts and suicidal tendencies out of each speaker. He pulled the camouflage cap down low to conceal his face. He slowed the SUV to a stop at the security check gate. He lowered the dark tinted window so he could be seen. A young white male military police officer approached the SUV with a clip board in his hands. On his side rested a Sig Sauer .9 millimeter.

"How's it going?" Ralo asked, taking charge of the conversation.

"I'm ok. Identification please," the MP requested with his hand out.

"Sure is hot out here ain't it," Ralo pretended to wipe sweat off his forehead with his hand, before passing him a dead man's ID. The MP looked at the identification card then glanced up at Ralo. He was just about to ask a question that Ralo felt would've blown his cover.

"Hey Jason!" two beautiful women hollered out at the same time. They were riding in a convertible red mustang with the top down waiting to exit the premises. The MP turned around and blushed. He started walking towards the mustang then he abruptly stopped and turned around.

"Here you go—," he looked down at the name on the ID, "Desmond, have a nice day," he handed Ralo the identification card back and went to entertain the two lovely ladies.

He pressed a button in the control picket and allowed a homicidal killer inside of the Army compound. The gate slowly rolled open and Ralo eased the stolen black tinted up Yukon through. He'd been on the base a couple of times before with Mellissa, so he knew his way around a little bit.

Mellissa was a freckled face redhead he met one day at Burger King. One thing led to another, and before you knew it, he had her begging for his nigger cock. The more Ralo banged her guts in, the looser her lips became. She told him all her boyfriend's illegal activities. Her boyfriend Benny was stealing guns off the train when the military shipment came in. His homeboy, Ronald, was the lieutenant over guns and ammo.

He placed all orders passed down from the major, along with extras for Benny to steal. Once the shipment arrived, Benny would break into the containers and steal two weapons out of each crate. Then when the train car was unloaded, Ronald was there with the shipping and receiving invoice which she altered. They'd been robbing the government for months. Now it was time for Ralo to rob their ass.

Ralo reversed the Denali. into a parking spot by the gym. He lowered each sun visor down to block the view from the front windshield. The rest of the windows were covered with 5% tint, so it was impossible to see in. Mellissa told him to park anywhere and call her when he was outside. Right when he was about to call her. He noticed a young sexy blond in black leggings, and a matching Nike sports bra.

She was waving in his direction. Ralo looked around to see who she was waving at. Nobody was in the vicinity but him. She continued to wave closing in the distance between her and the SUV. He cracked the window and waved back before slowly pulling away. Her wave stopped in mid motion, as a dumbfounded look spread across her face.

Ralo couldn't let a pretty blond spoil his plan. Careful not to draw anymore unwanted attention to himself, he found a nice parking spot under a tree located at the back of the firing range. Different caliber handguns, assault weapons, rifles were heard firing all at once. The sound of shooting echoed loudly through the air. Ralo gazed around a couple of times then called Mellissa.

"Hello," Mellissa answered on the second ring.

"I'm outside," he said, looking in each side mirror.

"Marcus is that you? Are those guns I hear in the background. Oh my God are you ok Marcus? Where are you at?" Mellissa rattled on without listening to a word he said. "Marcus can you hear me?" she looked down at her phone.

"I said I'm outside. I'm in the back-parking lot under the tree," Ralo said, getting frustrated with dealing with her stupid ass. Mellissa was dumber than Kelly Bundy.

"Why do I hear guns shooting Marcus?" Mellissa asked, calling him by the fake name he gave her two months ago.

"I'm in the back of the firing range. I'm at your job Mellissa, come outside," he explained holding back his foul choice of words.

"Ohhhh! Ok, here I come," she ended the call after finally realizing he was outside in the parking lot.

Ralo fired up the half of sherm that was in the ashtray. Two slow drags and he thumped the cigarette butt out the window. He put the .9mm Ruger inside of the center console. He glanced up and saw Mellissa struggling with a big black duffle bag. He peeped around the parking lot and noticed she was the only person outside, which was a good thing. He opened the passenger door.

"Hey Marcus," she grunted, struggling to lift the heavy duffle bag onto the front seat. "I done everything you asked me to do. I got the guns from my boyfriend," Mellissa volunteered information loudly standing outside of the SUV.

"Shut the fuck up and get in. Damn, you gonna tell everybody what we doing," Ralo snapped aggressively, peeping around to see if they'd drawn any attention.

Mellissa sat in the passenger seat with her head down and both hands in her lap. Ralo unzipped the bag. A big grin wormed across his face.

He reached over and raised her chin up, "Baby you done good."

"I told you. I told you I would get them, it was real easy. My boyfriend doesn't even know I took them. Marcus, can you give me some of that big black dick now. Please!" Mellissa begged, sucking on her finger.

"Yea, get in the back and take your clothes off," he ordered, toying with the weapons and ammunition in the bag. He caressed his hands over a FN .57 pistol equipped with a silencer. He checked the clip and saw that it was fully loaded. He jacked a round into the chamber and sat it down on the bag.

"Come on Marcus, my pink pussy is waiting on your cock," Mellissa said lustfully rubbing her clit.

"Turn around you lil' white bitch!" Ralo ordered crossing over the console hopping in the back. "Bend over you whore," Ralo pulled his pants down and his penis stood up to the occasion.

"Put it in my ass Marcus. I want to feel that black pole in my asshole," she reached back and spread her butt cheeks.

Ralo spit all over her rectum then forced his mushroom dick head inside. He spit in her ass again, working his full length all the way down to the nuts.

"Ahhhh, Marrrrcus."

"Shut up bitch and take this dick," he slammed deeper in her butt. "I know you like this dick white bitch," he grunted pounding with force.

"Yeeees Yeeees Yeeees! Fuck me harder Marcus! Fuck me harder! Give me all of that nigger cock," Mellissa yelled out, taking nine inches up her ass as if it was nothing. "Fuck me with that nigger dick. Fuck me nigger," she aggressively moaned out racial slurs.

Ralo pounded in her asshole like he was trying to split her in two. "Take this dick you nasty bitch," Ralo said between breaths.

He was tired of Mellissa calling him nigger every time they had sex. At first, he thought it was innocent. But each time they had a session, she would get more comfortable with saying it.

Ralo was fed up with the dingy whore bitch anyway. He got what he wanted, and he knew Mellissa would fold under pressure. Therefore, he had no choice but to cover his own ass.

"I'm finna cum bitch," Ralo grunted, feeling the lovely sensation about to explode.

"Cum in my ass nigger! Come in my ass you black nigger!" Mellissa yelled with her head banging up against the back door.

"Ahhhh, I'm cumming bitch," Ralo said through clench teeth. He reached for the FN .57 with the silencer-attached and fucked her again. He squeezed off two shots to the back of her head.

Ralo darted his eyes in every direction. The parking lot was still empty. The suppressor muffled the shots. Plus, they'd probably wouldn't have been heard because of all the shooting on the gun range. He pulled up his pants and jumped back into the driver's seat. He zipped up the duffle bag. Mellissa was slumped over the backseat. He reached back and pulled her down to the floorboard. He threw the big duffle bag on top of her body. Ralo sat there gripping the steering wheel tightly with both hands. He looked at himself in the rearview mirror and sneered. He only had two tasks left. One, making it back through the security gate without getting caught. Two, getting rid of Mellissa's body.

Ralo turned the air conditioner on high then lowered all the windows halfway allowing the smell of ass to escape. He sparked up the last sherm preparing himself for whatever may jump off. His mind was already made up. He was driving through the gate by choice or by force. One way or the other he was leaving. Rolling out alive in the Yukon or rolling out dead on a stretcher. Ralo saw Jason as he approached the security gate. He powered the driver's side window almost halfway down.

"I see you like your women all flavors huh?" Ralo said, referring to the black and white girls in the red mustang. "Which one makes your tongue wet?" he asked, passing the dead man's ID to the MP.

"Been liking chocolate since I was small," Jason said smiling.

He remembered the man in the black tinted up Yukon Denali. He held the ID in his hand. "Never had a chance to taste it though," he rubbed a hand over his face before buzzing the gate open.

"It tastes just like chocolate ice cream. And I know you done heard the saying," Ralo said, playing his role with the FN .57 pistol held low in his left hand.

"Yea! Once you go black you never go back," Jason responded with a laugh, handing Ralo the identification card back.

"That's right! Holla at you Jason," Ralo drove away leaving Jason standing there lost in his own thoughts.After an hour driving around the southside of Killeen looking for an isolated area to dispose of the body, Ralo became agitated and impatient. He drove a street over right behind his own warehouse. He parked in an empty lot of an abandoned building. The waist tall grass and debris from illegal dumping, made the spot perfect. Gangsta Nip's south park psycho purred throughout the sound system.

"I told yo dumb ass bitch," Ralo said out loud, putting everything he brought with him inside of the duffle bag. "Look at you, now! You stupid fuck!" he laughed at his imitation of Tony Montanta.

He gazed around making sure he didn't leave anything behind. "Catch you later bitch," he smirked, stepping out of the SUV.

He reached back inside and removed his .9mm from the center console. Ralo dropped the duffle bag down on the ground and peered at his surroundings. He picked up a long sturdy branch. He looked around until his eyes spotted an old dried up piece of cloth material. He tore the cloth in half making one long piece. He gazed around again then unscrewed the cap from the gas tank. He tied the long piece of cloth to the end of the branch. He eased the branch down into the gas tank. He took one last look around. He casually pulled a cigarette lighter out of his front pocket. He lit the end of the cloth. He turned around, grabbed the duffle bag and sprinted full speed to his warehouse over on the next street.

Ralo made it to the warehouse right before the SUV blew up... BOOOOM! The explosion rocked the entire tin building. He sat the bag of guns on the table in front of the flat screen television. Beads of sweat raced down his face. Ralo walked out of the front door hopped in his 1985 Buick Regal and got ghost. He wasn't about to stick around just to find anything out. No evidence. No confession. No case. He laughed at the thought as he drove to his next destination.

$$$

Tron and Lil' Brandon traveled I45 North with 10 books (KILO'S OF COCAINE) concealed in a compartment underneath the backseat of the Dodge Ram 3500. Tron normally took the trip alone like always. But Lil' Brandon had been asking him about making some extra money for a month. He agreed to break Lil' Brandon off $500 dollars for each book he sold. So instead of moving the bricks for $28,000 like always. He added an extra $500 on the back end for delivery fee.

"Put that blunt out until we get up outta Jasper," Tron said, reducing his speed to 30 mph like the sign ordered. "We don't need to give these crackers no probable cause to search the truck. You feel me?" he cut his eyes at Lil' Brandon.

Tron had always tried to think ahead before problems occurred. Being smart was really paying off for him. He'd been successfully hustling in the game for over 20 years without going to jail.

"Ain't this the town where that nigga got drugged down the street," Lil' Brandon asked, referring to the James Byrd incident that happened in 1996. Lil' Brandon took one last hit then thumped the blunt out the window. He reached for the damn air freshener and sprayed it once, eliminating the snow cookie smell instantly.

"Yea, them dick suckin' ass peckerwoods! They tied a rope around his hands and dragged him for miles with a truck." Tron voiced, gazing down at the speedometer. "That was some fucked up ass shit," he stressed reaching for his cellphone. He texted a dude name Reed letting him know that he was five minutes away.

"Man, I'm glad I don't stay out here," Lil' Brandon replied looking out the window.

"Say B, get three of those books from the back," Tron's eyes peeped each mirror then back down at the speedometer. Going over the speed limit was the quickest way to get stopped in Jasper.

"Bet!" Lil' Brandon hopped in the back. He pulled the bottom of the backseat forward, and it folded down flat. He opened the concealed compartment that was built into the bottom half of the seat. He removed three kilo's and closed the compartment then folded the seat back to original form.

"Get the strap from underneath my seat and stay in the back. Any shady shit pop his fuckin top. You hear me B?" Tron asked, making eye contact with him through the rearview mirror. "There he goes right there," he pointed to the chubby dude walking down the steps of an old run-down house with a backpack on his back.

"Done deal!" Lil' Brandon slid a bullet into the chamber and sat right behind the passenger seat. The .44 Bulldog was staring at the back of the seat ready to bark. Tron parked in front of the house.

"Tron, what's up bro," Reed said, as soon as he opened the door. "I didn't think you was coming," he continued, closing the door shut.

"You know when money calls, I rise for the occasion. You got your funds in order?" Tron asked, killing the small talk.

"Always bro!" Reed leaned forward and took off the backpack. "Here you go, count it," he handed Tron the backpack.

"You been straight every time we did business" Tron opened the backpack and dumped all the money into the center console and handed the bag back. Tron nodded at Lil' Brandon through the rearview mirror.

"What the-!" Reed uttered out, when Lil' Brandon handed him the first brick of cocaine. "Bro! Bro!" he couldn't get his words out correctly from being alarmed. Reed was unaware of anyone else being in the truck when he got inside. He shook his head and placed the brick in his backpack. Lil' Brandon handed him the remaining two.

"Hit me up whenever you're ready," Tron said before shaking his hand.

"Will do hustler," Reed replied, looking back over the seat at Lil' Brandon shaking his head. He jumped out with the backpack in his hand and walked back towards the house.

"Scary ass nigga," Lil' Brandon laughed, and got back into the front seat.

"He's far from scary Lil' B. He was just too comfortable. You can never get to comfortable in this line of work. You feel me? Gotta stay on note at all times," Tron looked both ways twice before he proceeded through the stop sign.

The next two drops went exactly the same way...SMOOTH. That was the easiest $5,000 dollars Lil' Brandon ever made in his whole life. They jumped back on I45, but this time going North, hopping off on I35. Lil' Brandon sparked up another blunt laced with Snow Cookie. The sounds of Kevin Gates vibed throughout the truck. Gates was expressing very deeply how he was getting it out of the mud. Tron related to each and every word, it was like Kevin Gates was reading his mind. Lil' Brandon passed the blunt bobbing his head. He was thinking about his girl KeKe.

A couple of blunts later they were back in K town (Killeen). Tron noticed a few helicopters flying above as soon as he exited the highway.

"What do you think that's about?" Lil' Brandon asked, looking up at the sky through the front windshield.

"Ain't no telling B," Tron answered, wondering the same question himself.

He turned on Estes Drive, a block over from the warehouse. KP's (Killeen Police) were everywhere. He made a right on South Cambell were the spot was at. Two police cars blocked off the street. Tron glanced over at Lil' Brandon and told him to act normal. The truck was legit, he had license and insurance. Tron also had a permit to carry a concealed weapon. The only thing he was worried about had a bunch of dead president's faces on it. And that was $330,000 thousands reasons to be shook up. Money laundering and tax invasion was a federal case he didn't need.

"Let me do all the talking B," Tron inhaled then exhaled as the police officer approached his side of the truck. The police officer motioned with his hand to lower the window. Tron obeyed.

"Where are you guys headed?" the officer asked, as his eyes rapidly scanned the inside of the truck for probable cause to conduct a search.

"To that warehouse right over there," Tron pointed, placing his hands back on the steering wheel. "What's going on?

"That's what were here trying to find out. Where you boys coming from?" the officer asked, looking at Lil' Brandon.

"We coming from Houston. Now can we go? Or are we under arrest?" Tron said sternly, not breaking eye contact.

"Let'em through Jake," the officer yelled out. "Don't you boys be blowing up no cars," the officer said as they drove away. He watched them pull into the parking lot of the warehouse. They both got out of the truck and walked inside.

"What them hoes talking about kinfolk," Bug asked, locking the door back. "They been out there for about two hours," Bug peeked out the window again.

"He told us don't be blowing up no more cars. Whatever the fuck that supposed to mean," Tron replied, sitting down.

"I know I ain't leaving until them hoes leave," Lil' Brandon said sitting down next to Tron on the couch.

"What's in this bag?" he asked Bug.

"That shit was here when I walked in earlier," Bug answered, blazing up a sherm walking towards the table. He pulled on the sherm twice and passed it to Lil' Brandon.

Bug unzipped the bag and his eyebrows raised. The bag was filled with all kinds of automatic weapons. They all looked at each other before Bug zipped the bag closed.

"Can't be nobody but Ralo stupid ass," Bug stressed shaking his head.

"What if the laws would've followed our ass in here," Tron voiced, looking at Bug then Lil' Brandon.

He knew Ralo was playing a dangerous game with his life. He also knew Ralo wasn't playing with a full deck. And before he took a fall for a dumb ass nigga who didn't give a fuck. Some changes had to take place...and quickly.

$$$

CHAPTER 9

"BITCHES BITCHES BITCHES"
(GALLERIA MALL)
HOUSTON, TEXAS

Fast Blacc was on his way to the Galleria mall to cop himself a few Neiman Marcus caps. Mona had been blowing up his phone constantly ever since their last lick. Mona worked at a paint and body shop in South Park (a neighborhood). Jack's was well known around Houston for the best sprayed candy paint job on vehicles. Any automobile that came out of Jack's paint and body shop was above perfection.

Mona worked the front desk. She answered all calls, received all payments, and set all appointments. She also knew of every car that had a secret stash spot, along with its code and location.

"Yea!" Fast Blacc answered his cellphone on the first ring.

"Yeah! What the fuck you mean yeah? I been calling yo bitch ass for three mutha fuckin' days. Where is my mutha fuckin' money black ass nigga?" Mona hollered.

"Meet me at the Gallo bitch. I'll be in Macy's parking lot. And hurry the fuck up," Fast Blacc calmly said, observing traffic on 610 South freeway. He ended the call before she had a chance to say anything smart.

"Bitch ass nig-!" that was all Mona got out of her mouth before her ear heard the dial tone.

Fast Blacc knew he was neglecting Mona, but he had to show her who was running things. The traffic on 610 South began to get congested the closer he got to the Galleria area. Westhimer Street was two exits away. Traffic was moving at a slow pace. He reached for the sherm that sat in the air conditioner vent chilling, wrapped in a piece of aluminum foil. He opened the foil and placed the cold feeling filter between his lips. He magically removed the filter with his teeth. And since traffic was screwed up, Fast Blacc decided to get slowed down with it.

POOF! He fired up the liquid drug and instantly escaped. Being in stop and go traffic was more tolerable floating on cloud nine. Fat Pat lyrically rhymed about turning dreams into reality as the bass pounded. The 45-minute wait in traffic shot by. Between the good gorilla piss from Cali, and the jamming sounds of Fat Pat, 45 minutes felt like ten. Fast Blacc felt his phone vibrated in his hand. He gazed at the number and shook his head.

"Yea!" he answered, muting the sound system.

"I'm in Macy's parking lot," Mona said bothered, because her air conditioner wasn't working in her Toyota Camry.

"I don't see your ass. What kind of car you in?" he joked, exiting the freeway.

"Bitch ass nigga! I ain't got time to play no mutha fuckin' games with yo black ass. Its hot ass fuck out here. Where you at?" Mona snapped, looking around the parking lot fanning herself with a Hip-Hop Weekly magazine.

"Girl, I'm in Macy's parking lot now you trippin'. What mall are you at?" Fast Blacc played with her mind as he turned into Macy's parking lot.

"I'm at the Galleria. That's where you said to go," Mona was beyond pissed off. Sweat began to bead on her forehead from the fierce heat. She stepped out of her car.

"I said First Colony Mall. Not the Gallo you dumb bitch," Fast Blacc ended the call before she said her favorite three words.

He saw Mona standing outside of her car. Her cellphone was in her hand as she hollered at it. He smiled stopping his car right beside her.

Mona was so heated cursing at her cellphone, she didn't realize Fast Blacc was right next to her until he lowered his window.

"Get yo stupid ass in."

"What!" Mona barked with an attitude of a pregnant pit bull. She turned and locked eyes with Fast Blacc.

"Bitch ass nigga!" she served him her favorite words then got into his car. "You're a low down dirty mutha fucka," she vented, resting her head back on the headrest.

"You need to get that A/C fixed in that raggedy mutha fucka," he lowered the thermostat down to 60 degrees.

"If you pay me my mutha fuckin' money, I can do a lot of things," she replied, fanning her shirt rapidly against her body. Mona adjusted the air conditioner vent so that it blew directly on her.

"Bitch, you lucky I cut for your ass," he admitted, digging into one of his pockets pulling out three rolls of cash. He handed Mona the money. "I got a lil' something else for you too," Fast Blacc reached over and opened up his glove compartment. He grabbed the 24-karat solid gold necklace with a gold and diamond pacifier piece attached. It was the only physical evidence that linked him to the murder of Peewee. He handed it to Mona.

"Don't think you getting some pussy for this," she smiled batting her eyelashes. The princess cut diamonds sparkled in her eyes from the nipple of the pacifier. Mona placed the necklace around her neck.

"You got some good pussy, but not that damn good," he said seriously. "Just keep the licks coming so we can get this money," he cut his eyes at her twirling the chain with her finger.

"Ok, I'll hit you when I get another one," she said stepping out of his car into the sweltering heat. "Fuck this! I'm getting my A/C fixed today," she looked at Fast Blacc before closing his door.

Fast Blacc watched as Mona hopped into her vehicle and drove away. He sat contemplating on whether he would have to kill her or not. He hated leaving trails behind, because capital murder was a case not to be played with. One pair of loose lips could sink the whole ship. And Fast Blacc wasn't about to drown with the rest of the crew. He put his car into gear and drove to the Galleria entrance.

He ran into the Neiman Marcus store and purchased five different color caps. His next stop was First Colony Mall in Sugarland, Texas. He wanted to splurge on himself and knock off some fly units and shoes. He hopped back on the freeway taking 610 North to US 59 South, headed to Sugarland, Texas.

$$$

CHAPTER 10

"MACK MODE"
(TEXAS RELAYS)
AUSTIN, TEXAS

Bug left the warehouse in route to the Texas Relay's in ATX (Austin, TX). The relays were basically a big track meet were different colleges came together to compete against each other. Bug made it his duty to show up every year if he wasn't busy or locked up. The Texas Relays had so many beautiful fine women who attended, it was hard to focus your eyes on just one.

The parking lot was jumping, packed with cars and sexy fine women of all races. Bug cranked up his sound system to draw attention to himself. Like driving a snow white 750i sitting on 26-inch chrome Ashanti rims wasn't enough. Most of the women in the parking lot was goose necking trying to see who was driving.

Courtesy of the mirror tinted windows; all they saw was a reflection of their self. Bug smiled as the music pounded loud throughout the parking lot. He found a place to park and maneuvered the big body Beemer in backwards. Car alarm after car alarm sounded off because of the loud bass. He pulled out a gram of Tony Montana and snorted a couple of hits up each nostril. He checked and made sure his nose was clean in the rearview mirror before getting out of the car.

Bug stood 6 foot even, weighing 215 pounds. He wore a low caecar cut taper faded with circular waves. His edge up was so sharp, Steve Harvey would've been jealous. His skin was the color of a snicker bar.

On his feet he wore a pair of orange and white 95 Air Max. He had on a pair of white Coogie cargo shorts, and an orange Polo shirt with a white horse. Both wrist, ears and neck sparkled, along with his pinky finger. He felt the stares but kept his cool and strutted to the field like a real playa. He worked the scene with his eyes instead of rubber necking like the other nigga's around him. Everywhere he gazed there was an ass staring at him. Bug rubbed a hand unconsciously over his freshly groomed mustache and beard. He was lost in thought lusting over a sexy fine yellow bone. She was bending over tying one of her shoes. When she stood up, her butt swallowed the tight spandex material. Her butt was so smooth looking and round, Bug couldn't stop gawking.

"You like something you see?" a female asked standing behind him watching as he lusted over her roommate.

"I just might. Why, what's up? That's your girlfriend or something," Bug smiled before turning around facing a beautiful captivating female. She had on a pair of white leggings with a camel toe so plump, he couldn't stop peeking at it.

"Yeah, that's my roommate. Are you feeling her?" the girl asked, pulling up her leggings even further. "What's your name?" she asked, checking him out again from head to toe.

"Bug." he responded glancing back at her roommate walking their way. "What's your name half pint?"

"Anetria." she laughed at his joke. "Hey Kiara, this is Bug," she introduced the two as Kiara walked up.

"I was wondering who his fine ass was. I saw him staring at my ass while I was tying my shoes. I thought he was another pervert running around like yesterday," Kiara explained, referring to an incident of a man taking pictures of women bending over.

"I'm far from that baby. But I do love a nice ass and a fat pussy," Bug stressed, looking at Kiara then back at Anetria. They both giggled and looked at each other.

An hour later after Kiara's last race, Bug followed them home. They lived in a nice colony style home. He pulled into the driveway behind them then got out of his car. He made sure his strap went along with him. Bug watched the two fine freaks as they walked together. He pictured himself fucking Kiara's round ass from the back. They all walked in the house. Bug noticed it was really cold, which was cool with him. Their pad was laid. It looked like everything was brand new.

"Bug, you can have a seat on the couch if you want," Kiara offered, heading straight for to the bathroom.

"Hey Bug, you want something to eat or drink?" Anetria hollered from the kitchen.

"Yea, a soda and a slice of that fat ass pussy," he hollered back over his shoulder. He took the .9mm ruger out from behind his back and slid it underneath the cushion of the couch.

"You might not be able to handle this boy," she walked into the living room and handed him a cold 23 flavors.

"I know I can," he opened the can soda and drank half before sitting it down on the end table. "Let's see what your fine ass talking about," Bug took charge.

He laid Anetria down on the couch and kissed her. Her lips were soft, and her tongue tasted like juicy fruit gum. Bug wormed his tongue around her mouth as his hand rubbed the warm mound between her legs. Anetria moaned out. Bug removed her white leggings and met miss camel toe up close. He sat her up and took off her shirt. Her young chocolate breast eyed him. Anetria pulled his shirt over his head and was amazed by his ripped-up physic. She rubbed her hands down his solid torso sucking air through her teeth making a hissing sound.

"Stand up," Anetria ordered licking her lips. Bug stood up and kicked off his shoes.

She kneeled on the couch in front of him and undid his shorts. She snatched them down and his pole popped out and hit her on the nose. She giggled then attacked the super king-sized Snicker bar. Her moans floated throughout the room as she worked his length with skills of a prostitute.

She sucked and stroked his member with both hands. She spit a glob of saliva on his dick and slurped it back into her mouth. Bug grunted as she went down further deep throating his 9-inch cock.

"Damn girl, you just couldn't wait for me huh?" Kiara questioned, with a terry cloth towel wrapped around her body.

Her fresh scent invaded their nostrils enhancing both of their sexual lust. Kiara gaped at Bug's rock-hard shiny nightstick and let the towel drop to the floor.

"I couldn't talk I had a mouthful," Anetria bit down on her bottom lip. She worked his dick slowly in her hand as it throbbed.

"Girl, what does it taste like?" Kiara wondered, biting down on her bottom lip. She walked over and kissed Anetria passionately.

"Mmmmm! Sweet like chocolate," she placed her hand on top of Anetria's and helped her stroke his thickness. She placed the head of his penis in her mouth and circled her tongue around it as she sucked the tip.

"Ooooo shit!" Bug grunted.

Anetria joined the escapade and licked the bottom of his dick. She sucked on his balls tenderly.

"Ooooo, Ooooo!" he moaned out louder. Once they felt his body tense, their tongues stopped. They stared at his snake as it moved like a king cobra.

"Sit down," Kiara ordered, not taking her eyes off his cock. She straddled Bug reverse cowgirl style. She grabbed ahold of his thickness and worked the head inside her wetness.

"Ohhhh! Ohhhh!" Kiara moaned out softly, sliding down the length of his pole. Once she got adjusted to his size, she began to ride like a true cowgirl. She guided her pussy up and down coating his pole with her juices. "You like this pussy?" she asked above a whisper, as she worked her coochie up to the tip and back down to his nuts.

"Yee- Yea!" Bug stammered out. He held her waist and thrusted deeper inside of her. Her wetness and how tight her walls were, had him about to explode. Kiara eased off his dick as she was cumming. She turned around and positioned her plump vagina in front of his face.

Anetria wasted no time sucking and licking Kiara's juices off Bug's cock. She waited patiently for her turn to ride the pleasure pole. Her pussy was so soaked Bug slid right inside. Anetria inched her way down and grinded in a circular motion. She felt his love muscle probing in her stomach. Anetria leaned forward and darted her tongue around Kiara's rectum. Bug had her ass spread, sucking and licking her to ecstasy. Kiara rode Bug's face like a brand-new bicycle on Christmas morning. She came in his mouth twice already, not including the two times when she was riding his dick.

"Ooooo Ooooo! Ohhhh, I'm about to cum. Ahhhh, Ahhhh," Kiara hollered out grabbing ahold of Bug's head squeezing with her thighs. She came all in his mouth, and Bug continued to vacuum up her juices.

"FUCK!" she yelled out, jumping off Bug's face. Her knees were weak as she kneeled down and returned the anal favor to Anetria.

"Ohhhh Kiara! Sssss, Mmmmm. I'm finna cum too," Anetria cried out bouncing up and down Bug's dick.

"Yeah just like that. Ride that dick. Ride it, ride it," Bug said through clenched teeth.

Anetria wasted no time sucking and licking Kiara's juices off Bug's cock. She waited patiently for her turn to ride the pleasure pole. Her pussy was so soaked Bug slid right inside. Anetria inched her way down and grinded in a circular motion. She felt his love muscle probing in her stomach. Anetria leaned forward and darted her tongue around Kiara's rectum. Bug had her ass spread, sucking and licking her to ecstasy. Kiara rode Bug's face like a brand-new bicycle on Christmas morning. She came in his mouth twice already, not including the two times when she was riding his dick.

He spread Anetria's ass and pumped faster. "Tighten that pussy. Ohhhh that's it," he felt Anetria squirt all over his dick.

He jabbed faster and faster pulling her forcefully down on top of him. "I'm finna bust," Bug grunted out.

"Get up girl, get up," Kiara said excitedly.

They both put their faces in his lap as Kiara stroked him until he blew up like the Challenger rocket. His cum shot all over their face.

"AHHHH!" Bug yelled out loudly, as they both took turns polishing his head until he pushed them away. They both laughed as he laid back on the sofa exhausted. It took him an hour to bust one nut. Every time he got ready to blow his load, one of them would switch positions. Bug was snoring five minutes later.

Anetria and Kiara took their show to the shower. They bathed and sucked one another until climax. After they showered, they crawled into bed and went to sleep also.

Bug was laid out on the couch the next morning dreaming. A pretty fine woman was riding his dick. The dream felt so real. He kept smelling bacon and eggs. Right when he started cumming, he woke up. His first sense to kick in was smell. He smelled breakfast cooking. He also felt wetness between his legs. He looked down and saw Kiara sucking his dick. She looked up at him and smiled.

Bug ended up staying two more days after that. And on the third day, he made himself leave. They were draining his nut sack dry. He was too tired to do anything but sleep.

Anetria and Kiara hated to see him go. They wanted to give him a going away treat, but Bug quickly declined the offer. He had to get back to the money. He'd promised to call 'em whenever he was free again. Bug hopped into his white ghost and smashed back to Killeen.

CHAPTER 11

"WHY ME"
(FEDERAL ROAD)
HOUSTON, TEXAS

Fast Blacc turned down his music as he pulled into the First Colony Mall parking lot. The candy blue slab on super pokers was enough attention. He parked his car in the back of the parking lot away from others. He jumped out admiring his ride with a sneer on his face. He walked towards the mall entrance. He activated his security alarm and the convertible top raised up and secured itself shut. He strode across the parking lot with a slight limp in his left leg from being shot several years ago. Fast Blacc looked to his right and noticed security turning around peering his way. He shook his head and kept walking. The day was too sunny for a busta rent-a-cop to stop his shine. He watched as people were coming and going inside of the mall. Every face he peeped had a smile on it. He opened the door and let it close on a woman behind him. She mumbled something under her breath.

The inside of the mall carried a totally different vibe. It was the beginning of July. School was out, and kids ran all over. The air felt good as it flowed over his hot skin. Different food smells molested his nostrils. Indistinct conversations traveled throughout the mall. Beautiful women strutted around with their boyfriends, husbands, tricks, sugar daddies, girlfriends, or alone. Fast Blacc looked at every fat ass coming and going.

He dipped inside of a Foot Locker and knocked off five pair of kicks. One for each Neiman Marcus cap he bought. He paid cash at the register, making the young female cashier eyes bulge at the numerous rolls of currency. Fast Blacc noticed her eyes were moving faster than her hands was ringing up his purchase. He tipped her a c-note and her jaw almost hit the floor. He grabbed his bags off the counter and left. He felt the young broad watching him as he walked away. He turned up his swag and tilted his blue Los Angeles Dodger cap to the right side and strutted harder.

Fast Blacc stood outside of the Foot Locker deciding where to go to next. He gazed around and zoomed in on a short and sexy paper sack brown colored female. She was inside of an African Boutique rear-ranging merchandise on a shelf. He eased his way towards the Boutique. The closer he got the sexier she became.

The girl stood about 5'2". She had to weigh about 140 pounds as fat as her backside was. Her skin glowed. Her hair laid fully on her shoulders. Her lips favored the actress Megan Goode. Her eyes were big and brown. She had an exotic appeal about herself, like she was from another country. Fast Blacc walked into the African Boutique and pretended to look at the African Art.

He was looking at the girl so hard, she glanced up at him. He quickly sat down his Foot Locker bags, picked up an item from the shelf, and examined it like he was really interested. He stole a peek in her direction, only to realize she was gone.

"Excuse me sir! Are you interested in anything?" a woman asked from his blind side.

"N'all, I'm just looking," he responded, looking around wondering where the short and sexy female went.

"Boy you know damn well you don't want nothing in here," she said, looking him over from head to toe.

"What!" he snapped, then spun around. He stared into the pretty brown eyes of the girl he was just looking for. "How do you know what I want?" he questioned, looking down at her aqua green nails.

"I saw your black ass watching me when you came out of Foot Locker. You know how many lame dudes I turn down a day?" she quizzed, straightening a statue on a top shelf.

"I don't give a damn about how many nigga's you turn down; you hear me?" he stepped closer in her space, peeking down at her name tag pinned on her shirt. "All I'm worried about is me. And what I can do to keep a smile on your face," Fast Blacc adjusted his cap on his head.

"I like that, you're very original," she smiled with a perfect set of white teeth.

"What's your name?" he asked, gazing at the two-carat diamond earrings in each of her earlobes.

"Look here! If you wanna talk to me, you gotta keep it real. You already know my name. So, miss me with that high school shit. I saw you peeping my name tag. So, what's your name?" she said, bringing a smile to his face.

She usually didn't entertain dudes at work. But he was handsome to her for a dark skin man.

"Everybody calls me Fast Blacc. But you can call me whatever you want Lyric," he said with a slight grin, looking down at her name tag once more.

"Hey, check this out. I get off in a couple of more hours, meet me out front. I gotta get back to work before I get fired. I don't like to be kept waiting neither. You hear me, Fast Blacc," Lyric stressed, before continuing back to work.

She went about her job details with dick on her mind. It's been close to a year since her last sexual encounter with a man. Besides a hot wet tongue, her fingers, and a stiff rubber dildo, she went without. However, her pussy wasn't having it today. Lyric was craving for a big long fat hard dick.

Fast Blacc casted a glance down at his gold blue face Rolex, laced with blue diamonds. It was 4 o'clock. He had a couple of hours to kill before he met back up with Lyric. He peered around at different department stores and his eyes locked in on the Victoria's Secret shop. An idea popped in his mind. He went to visit Victoria to find out more about her secrets. He was greeted upon entering the store.

"How are you doing young man?" A saleswoman asked, wearing a tight grey skirt and a satin white blouse with the first two buttons undone. She wore a pair of grey high heels, which made her a few inches taller than Fast

Blacc. Her clevege was so deep, he couldn't keep his eyes off of her breast. "How can I help you today?" she asked, adjusting her Versace eyewear.

"I'm just looking," he responded, watching her remove some strands of hair away from her face.

"Are you shopping for a wife or a girlfriend?" she inquired out of curiosity. She was an old freaky momma in her mid-40's who loved young thugs.

"N'all just a friend of mine," he looked down at her long silky looking legs.

"What do you have in mind? Something sexy? Or something more erotic?" she asked licking her glossy lips.

"I gotta go with sexy for right now," he stated, watching as she bent all the way over with ease to fold a pair of boy shorts on the lower display shelf.

"Do you see anything you like," her skirt inched its way up exposing her fat pussy in a lavender thong. She looked back and saw him rubbing on himself. "I take that as a yes," she stood up and smiled, looking down at the bulge in his pants.

"Let me get the same set you got on," he adjusted his hard on.

"You better make sure the lucky lady takes care of that," the saleswoman flirted heavily, as she indiscreetly squeezed his manhood.

"I'm sorry, but I forgot to ask what size does she wear?"

"I don't know. But her ass is a little fatter than yours. Her titties are that size," he pointed to a mannequin in the front window.

"Ok, I know just the right size. Meet me at the back register while I wrap up your purchase," she pointed before disappearing into the back.

"Old ass super freak," Fast Blacc said to himself. He walked back to the cash register and waited.

He thought about fucking Lyric's little sexy ass. He pictured himself sexing her froggy style like Ving Rhimes did Baby Boy's momma. He really wanted to feel those plump lips smacking on his dick while he looked into her pretty brown eyes.

"Will this be cash or charge?" the saleswoman questioned, placing the neatly wrapped box on the counter. She watched as he pulled out a roll of money with a rubber band around it. "That'll be forty-three dollars, and seventy cents," she informed him.

"Here, keep the change," Fast Blacc handed her a hundred dollar bill.

"Thank you!" she passed him a receipt and a card with her name and number on it. "Don't be scared to use it," she said, winking her eye.

"Bet!" he walked away feeling more playa than he already was. He thought about coming to First Colony Mall more often.

He faded a couple more stores and scooped up about 10 units. He walked back to his car and put everything on the back floor. He kept the Victoria's Secret bag to impress Lyric when he met back up with her. And if everything went the way he'd expected, Lyric would be cumming on his dick by nightfall.

He looked down at his $50,000 time piece and saw it was almost 6 o'clock. Fast Blacc strutted his way back to the African Boutique. He was 10 minutes early. His old man taught him that the early birds gets the worm. However, in this case, the early nigga gets a new piece of pussy. He chuckled at the thought. He posted up by a cotton candy stand next to the African Boutique. A few minutes rolled by and out came Lyric. Fast Blacc stood there watching her look around for him. As soon as she started to walk in the opposite direction, the smile evaporated from his face.

"Lyric!" Fast Blacc hollered out, catching up with her. She turned around when she heard her name.

"Boy, I told your ass don't keep me waiting," Lyric snapped with a feisty attitude. "Ain't nothing funny," she continued to walk away.

"I don't know why yo short ass frontin'. I was standing there watching you the whole time," he said, walking on the side of her. "You just walked out about two minutes ago," he cut his eyes down at her fat bubble butt. "Here this is for you," handing her the Victoria's Secret bag. "Just a lil' something you might like."

Lyric grabbed the bag and smiled. "Thanks! I see you're starting off on the right track. I gotta give you a plus for that," she bumped into him with her shoulder then smiled.

"So what's up? You wanna go someplace and chill?" he asked, without beating around the bush.

"Do I look like one of your little freaks," she glanced up at him waiting for an answer.

"Never said you was. I just wanted to go someplace and kick back. Maybe blow a couple of blunts and whatever," he suggested again, not giving up easily.

"Yea we can chill. But, you're gonna have to come to my place," she smiled up at him. Fast Blacc held the door open for her to walk through. "Oh, I see you're just a real gentleman," she said, with an even bigger grin on her face.

"If you only knew," he truthfully said, as he thought about her being face down ass up.

"Just follow me. I live ten minutes from here," Lyric informed him, getting into her money green convertible Thunderbird. She watched as Fast Blacc walked to his car isolated in the back of the parking lot. She wondered why he parked his car so far away. She shook her head and drove in his direction. Once he started up his car; he followed her to her place.

First Colony Homes were located off of US 59 freeway in Sugarland, Texas. Fast Blacc glanced up at the huge burnt orange sign which read "WELCOME TO FIRST COLONY HOMES". He trailed closely behind her looking at the expensive two-story miniature brick mansions. The landscaping was picture perfect, edged to perfection, trimmed to precision. After two more right turns and a left, Lyric turned into her driveway. Fast Blacc pulled in right behind her and parked. She waited until he stepped out of the car.

"Boy, bring your slow ass on," she said, unlocking the door to her two-story Mediterranean brick home. Lyric inherited $2 million when her dad died in a chemical plant explosion in Pasadena, Texas. She was only 15 years old at the time, so her inheritance sat in a bank account gaining interest until she turned 18. That was over 11 years ago.

"Take your shoes off if you don't mind," she kicked her shoes off.

"You got a nice lil' spot momma," he complimented looking around her place. He peeped a lot of African art as he removed his shoes in the foyer.

He stepped down into the living room area. His feet sunk into the thick white soft imported Persian carpet. Fast Blacc was impressed with his new prospect. He didn't know where Lyric would fit in, but he was most definitely keeping her around.

"Make yourself comfortable. The kitchen is right over there if you're thirsty. I'm finna take a shower and see if this fits," she held out the Victoria's Secret bag. He watched her disappear down the hallway.

Fast Blacc cast his eyes around her pad. Everything was top notch and lavish, including the 100-gallon fish aquarium. A big unique painting of Nefertiti the Egyptian queen hung over the fireplace. He sat down on the super soft plush sofa and kicked back with both arms spread across the top. He rested his feet on the table in front of him. His phone vibrated in his pocket. Pulling it out he glanced at the number and sucked his teeth. He'd wondered what the caller wanted this time.

"Yea!" he answered, not really wanting to be bothered. Lyric was the only thing on his mind at this particular moment.

"Damn pimp, been hittin' you up for three days. What's up?" the caller asked.

"Been busy man, what's the deal," he took his cap off and sat it beside him.

"I told you to make sure he was alone, whenever you made it happen. What was so hard about that," the caller stressed aggravated.

"Man fuck all that bullshit. As long as the job got done who gives a fuck," he raised his voice out of anger. He sat up on the sofa.

"I give a fuck pea brain ass nigga. I'm trying to keep my tracks covered. The other nigga in the car wasn't supposed to be touched," the caller on the other end voiced in a threatening tone.

"Fuck it! Two niggas for the price of one," Fast Blacc stood up and walked around.

"How could you fuck up something so simple?" the caller wondered.

"I didn't fuck shit up. Ralo fucked it up," he spoke loudly into his cellphone walking through the house.

"Ralo! Ralo! Why in the fuck did you use somebody more stupid than you," the caller hollered on the other end of the line. "Now the other nigga is laying up in the hospital."

"It don't matter who I sent to kill the nigga. Fuck him!" Fast Blacc vexed loudly, walking back and forth.

He was so deep into his conversation over the phone; he didn't see Lyric standing in the doorway listening to each and every word.

"Man, fuck the dumb shit. Stop calling my mutha fuckin' phone bitch ass nigga. Our business is done."

"When I catch yo-!" the caller tried to say, before Fast Blacc dismissed the call.

"Is everything alright?" Lyric asked, letting her presence be known. "I thought you had somebody up in my house. I heard you all the way in the bathroom," she stood in the doorway with her hands on her hips, standing back on her bowlegs. The lavender and white panty and bra set had her looking like one of the Victoria's Secret Angels. Her butt was visible through the gap between her legs.

"Yea I'm good, nothing for you to worry about," he totally forgot about the argument he just had once he laid eyes on her. He was speechless, but his dick had something to talk about as it throbbed in his pants.

"Come on, let's go to my room," Lyric told him, leading the way. Her butt jiggled with each step she took. Her brown skin shined from head to toe. Her sweet-smelling scent had his mouth watering. "Here's my comfort zone. You can take a shower in there," she pointed, grabbing the remote filling the room with the sexual old school sounds of Jodeci. Scented tropical candles burned throughout the room.

"Girl, yo young ass don't know nothing about that," Fast Blacc said, referring to Jodeci, as he stripped down to his Armani boxer shorts. He neatly folded his clothes and sat them on a chair that was sitting in the corner of the room.

"Boy please! Go wash that black dick and hurry up. My pussy is-so wet," she turned and walked sexually towards the super king size bed. Her bed sat up high with a two-step carpeted platform surrounding the bed. The mattress came up to her shoulders when she was standing. She sat down on the first step and waited.

Fast Blacc took a quick two-minute shower. He washed all his hot spots. Underarms, feet, nuts, and butt. He chuckled at the thought of the fast showers he took in prison. Where the water was hot in the summer, and cold in the winter. Inmates had two minutes or less to shower, and the water was shut off. He shook his head at the thought. He stepped out, dried off, and wrapped the towel around his waist. He grabbed his boxers and sat them on top of his clothes.

Lyric sat on the lower step surrounding her bed with her smooth brown legs crossed. Her thighs looked so good and thick; she could've put Popeye's out of business. She leaned back on both arms and uncrossed her legs. Fast Blacc stood in front of her and removed the towel from around his waist. Jodeci's greatest hits serenaded out of the surround sound speakers. It was time for Lyric to perform, and the microphone was right in her face.

She grabbed ahold of it and did a quick mic check. She smacked her full succulent lips on the head of his penis making him moan out. Lyric held his cock straight up, licking the bottom while she softly caressed his testicles with her other hand. His dick jumped in her hand anticipating the warmth of her mouth. As if reading his mind, Lyric placed his manhood in her mouth and went to work. She coated his pipe with saliva easing it down her throat. She came up for air then devoured his dick again. She stroked his rod with the intent to please.

Fast Blacc's moans filled the room. He sounded like he was singing back up for Jodeci. He pushed her head off his dick. Lyric looked up at him puzzled. He got down on his knees and crawled between her legs. She leaned back, opened her legs and invited his tongue in. He licked her inner thighs leaving a moist trail on each one. He toyed with her clitoris through her panties. Lyric gasped out from pleasure. He pulled her panties to the side and sampled her goods.

"Ooooo!" she moaned out, arching her back further.

She rested both elbows on the second step and spread her thighs even wider. "Ahhhh, that feels so good," she guided his head in the right spot. "Right there. Ooooo, Yeees!" she threw her head back.

Fast Blacc raised up and pulled her panties off. "Ummm! Ummm! Ummm!" he licked his lips then dove his tongue back into her honey pot. Her juices ran down her butt. He drove his middle finger into her rectum while sucking hard on her pearl tongue.

"Ohhhh shit! Ohhhh shit! I'm about to cum, I'm about to cum. Ahhhh, Sssss, Ahhhh!" Lyric hollered out cumming in his mouth.

She turned over and crawled up the second step into the bed. She picked up the remote control and the 50-inch screen came to life. She punched a few more buttons then she appeared on the flat screen sexy as ever. She removed her bra and licked each breast tenderly. Her hands began to roam all over her body. Fast Blacc stood there masturbating as she fingered her pussy until she came. She sucked her juices off her finger then offered him some.

"Ooooo Weeee! You freaky bitch," Fast Blacc said, jumping into the super king size playground. He grabbed her hand and licked her fingers clean. "Get on top of this dick," he ordered, laying back propping a couple of pillows behind him. This was his first time watching himself on a live flick. Lyric squirted some Hot Six oil over his penis and slid straight down with ease. Fast Blacc watched as she worked her fat round ass up and down to the sounds of Jodeci.

"COME AND TALK TO ME, I REALLY WANNA KNOW YOU. CAN I TALK TO YOU, I REALLY WANNA MEET YOU..." If KC would've saw Lyric working her pussy the way she was, he would've been next in line.

"Fuck me from the back so you can cum," Lyric spun around on his dick facing the big screen. She raised herself up slowly watching how long and fat his cock was. She jacked her plump ass in the air and looked right into the camera. "Fuck this pussy Fast Blacc," she voiced sexually, biting down on her bottom lip.

"That's what I'm talking about," he jumped up and mounted her from behind. Her pussy wrapped around his dick and squeezed. He held her around her waist and thrust deeply. He peered at the big screen and saw the seriousness on his face as he punished her coochie.

Lyric slammed back against him matching his strokes. "Ooooo Ooooo! I'm cumming on your dick. I'm cumming on your dick," she moaned out, looking directly into the camera.

She looked at herself then at Fast Blacc. Sweat poured down his face like a runaway slave. He felt the sensation creeping up his testicles. "I'm finna cum," he grunted. "I'm finna cum!" he groaned through clenched teeth. Lyric quickly turned around and positioned herself right in front of him.

"Cum in my mouth," she grabbed his manhood and jerked until he shot semen all over her face. Cum oozed down her eyes, nose, mouth, and dripped off her chin. She rubbed the cum all over her breast. She grabbed his dick and sucked it a few times for the camera.

"You're dick taste so fucking good," she smiled licking the corner of her mouth.

Fast Blacc laid on his back with both arms spread. His chest rose and fell as he blew air between his lips. "Girl, I can't lie," he said between breaths. "You got some-good ass pussy."

Lyric laughed and went to the bathroom. She cleaned herself up and came back out with a hot soapy towel. She looked over at Fast Blacc, he was knocked out. She cleaned him up, then crawled in the bed next to him. She didn't know she was actually sleeping with the devil, and the conversation she heard would cost her, her life.

$$$

CHAPTER 12

"WHY ME"
(FEDERAL ROAD)
HOUSTON, TEXAS

Hollywood cleaned her whole house from top to bottom. The place was actually spotless, but her mind was moving nonstop with thoughts of her brother Peewee. Therefore, cleaning was the first thing she did. She pondered who would've wanted her brother killed. As far as she knew he didn't have any enemies. Hollywood wasn't lame to the code of the streets. But when the game takes someone you love it's a different story. She wiped down the marble counter tops in the kitchen so many times, the once wet towel was completely dry. She looked around for anything dusty or dirty to keep her mind away from vindictive thoughts.

As soon as she stopped cleaning her brain churned revenge. Her brother's death ate away at her conscious. Deep down inside Hollywood felt she was the blame. Therefore, finding Peewee's killer was a must. She gazed around her home and forced a smile. Pictures of her and Redline were visible throughout the house. He was the only person in her life worth living for. She inhaled deeply, then exhaled slowly. After grief cleaning the entire house from top to bottom, the only thing left dirty was herself. She walked into the bathroom and peeled off her sweaty clothes and took a steaming hot shower.

Hollywood stood underneath the rain fall shower head enjoying the soothing water. She bathed her body twice before getting out. She dried off and wrapped a big terry cloth towel around her body. She looked in the mirror and rubbed her hair and scalp with some Hollywood beauty coconut oil moisturizer. Her hair was naturally long and thick. She put it in a neat ponytail. She applied some Dove deodorant under her armpits and rubbed Jergan's Natural Glow all over her body. She picked up her clothes and placed them inside of the dirty clothes hamper.

Stepping into her bedroom she selected a pair of baby blue thongs with a matching bra. Walking into the closet looking around, she settled on a pair of blue Mother Denim ankle skinnies with black double-sided stripes. She grabbed a white cotton low cut blouse and a black thin fitted tuxedo like jacket. She knew how cold hospitals were and she wanted to be prepared. She'd promised Redline that she would check up on Flagg.

Hollywood slid her freshly pedicured toes into a pair of black open toe platform heels. She glided on some L.A. Girl glossy lip gloss on her plump lips. Once she was satisfied with her gorgeous reflection. She grabbed the keys to her Lexus SUV and headed to Ben Taub Hospital.

$$\$\$\$$$

CHAPTER 13

"NEVER SAW IT COMING"
(HOBBY AIRPORT)
HOUSTON, TEXAS

Amber held her breath as the big 747 landed on the runway smoothly. This was her second time flying in her whole life Her first experience wasn't so great. The front tire blew out when the airplane touched the runway. The entire plane felt like it was about to fall apart. Amber told herself that she would never fly again after that. She loosened her grip on both armrest and exhaled blowing air out through her nostrils. She looked around at the other passengers. It was like she was the only nervous person on board. The airplane came to a complete stop.

She reached and grabbed her Louis Vuitton luggage from the overhead compartment. She exited the plane and was quickly blinded by the sunlight. Pulling down her Louie sunglasses she walked down the steps. Once her feet touched the ground, she extended the handle on the pull away luggage and made her way inside the airport.

The terminal was filled with people moving about like ants. Amber pulled her luggage swaying her voluptuous backside drawing unwanted attention. She passed through the security check point X-ray machine with no problems. Her Chloe' high rise jeans were so tight you could count the change she had in her pocket; her red bottom high heels click clacked on the hard floor as she headed for the exit. She stopped briefly to call Hollywood to let her know that she just landed. Amber ended the call once she found out Hollywood was at Ben Taub Hospital. She grabbed hold of her luggage and continuing towing.

"Excuse me! Do you need any help with that?" A short pretty brown skin female asked.

"What?!" Amber snapped, looking back over her shoulder to see who was talking to her.

"I asked do you need any help with that," she voiced again scanning Amber from head to toe.

"N'all I'm good. It rolls real easy," Amber replied, staring at her full lips.

"I'm not talking about your luggage. I'm talking about that," the girl stressed, pointing at Amber's thick round backside.

The girl smiled then sucked on her bottom lip while lusting on Amber's perfect shaped ass.

"Ain't no shame in your game huh?" Amber asked, feeling the tingling sensation between her legs from watching her suck on her luscious lips. "You just walk around looking for the fattest ass?" she wondered out of curiosity.

"Not the fattest ass, but the complete package," she said looking into Amber's hazel eyes. "What's your name?" her eyes ran over Amber's thick thighs.

"Amber! How about you?" she couldn't be still as she shifted her weight from one leg to the other. Amber was becoming real moist looking into her eyes as she toyed with her pretty lips.

"Lyric! But your fine ass can call me whatever you want. Where are you from?" she asked walking around Amber.

"I'm from Crockett," Amber put a hand on her hip. "Who are you here with?" she questioned, raising one of her eyebrows.

"I just dropped my girlfriend off. She's a stewardess," Lyric said truthfully.

"You don't waste any time huh?"

"Not when it comes to something I like," Lyric responded. "Where you headed to?"

"To the hospital. Why?" Amber asked, looking at her Gucci time piece.

"I can give you a ride if you want," Lyric offered, waiting for an answer. "What hospital you going to?"

"Ben Taub! Where the broke bitches go," Amber said, with a smile on her face. Her and Lyric shared their first real laugh together.

"Cool, I'm headed that way anyway," Lyric smiled. "Now do you need any help with that?"

"You just don't give up do you," Amber said turning around.

"I'm talking about this," Lyric grabbed the handle to Amber's luggage and led the way to her vehicle.

Amber smiled shaking her head following Lyric to the parking garage. She hit the remote control deactivating the alarm and automatically starting the car. Lyric placed Amber's luggage in the backseat. They both got into the money green Thunder Bird. Lyric turned the air conditioner on high and lowered the convertible top.

"You said Ben Taub Hospital, right?" Lyric asked, activating the navigation system.

"Yea that's it," Amber replied, reaching for her seatbelt.

She reclined her seat back and pulled her Gucci shades down over her eyes. "Just wake me up when we get there," she couldn't sleep on the airplane flight to Houston. Her phobia wouldn't allow her to close her eyes for even a second. She inhaled a deep breath of fresh air and stared up at the blue sky. Amber was asleep ten minutes later.

Lyric gazed at her while she was sleeping. Her eyes explored over Amber's well shaped curves and blemish free skin. The way her jeans hugged her coochie, Lyric almost rear ended a couple of cars on two different occasions. She shook her head and paid closer attention to where she was going. Lyric bobbed her head to the sounds of Travis Scott. The strong wind whipped through both of their hair. The downtown skyline was visible as she sped down highway 288 North.

Lyric thought back to her freak session with Fast Blacc, and how he startled her with his loud verbal phone conversation. She imagined Amber rolling around in her super king size bed with them. She cut her eyes in Amber's direction noticing she was still sleeping. Lyric smiled at the thought. She took the N. Macgregor exit and made a left turn at the traffic light. In a matter of minutes, she turned into Ben Taub's parking lot.

"Amber we're here," Lyric announced, placing the car into park looking at her. "Hey sleepy head!" she leaned over and placed a soft kiss on Amber's lips.

Amber woke up and looked around. "We're here already," ignoring the fact that she felt Lyric's soft full lips.

"Yea you slept the whole way here. You want me to wait for you or you're good," she said, raising up her Versace sunglasses and resting them on her head.

"N'all, I'm good. But thanks a lot for the ride. Put my number in your phone," Amber stretched out before raising her seat back up. "936-709-8435."

"Ok, I have you locked in," Lyric said, dialing the number right back. "That's me right there," she informed as Amber's cellphone rang.

"Alright, I'll call you. And thanks again," she stepped out of the car and reached in the backseat for her luggage. Amber looked around and pulled her luggage towards the entrance doors.

She felt Lyric's eyes roaming all over her body. She gazed back over her shoulder and smiled. And just like she thought, Lyric was shaking her head side to side with a hungry look on her face.

The automatic entrance doors divided in two as she walked into the hospital. Amber was greeted by the cold air as soon as the doors parted. Hollywood told her the floor and the room number, so she looked around until she located the elevator. She pushed the handle down on her luggage until it locked. She picked it up and made her way to the elevator. She pressed the up arrow and patiently waited.

Amber was rewarded less than a minute later. She moved aside and allowed several people to exit. Once they cleared out, she stepped inside and pressed the number 5. She rode up to the fifth floor trying to think of the last time she visited someone in the hospital. A bell chimed indicating her floor. She stepped off the elevator looking in both directions. Her eyes peered at the room numbers beside each door. She proceeded toward 507 then walked inside the room.

The room was colder than the rest of the hospital she walked through. A low beeping sound was heard coming from the monitors beside the bed. Amber saw a dark figure laid up. He looked frail. She walked up to the side of the bed and looked down at Flagg.

"I know we don't know each other, but I promised Redline I'd come and check up on you," Amber stressed, looking at the white plastic helmet covering his entire head. "I really don't know what to say. I pray and hope you get better."

"You and me both," Hollywood said walking out of the bathroom. Amber turned around startled with her hand over her heart. "Sorry about that, didn't mean to scare you," Hollywood smiled, extending her hand. "You gotta be Amber," Hollywood shook her hand firmly.

"Yea, and you must be Hollywood," she eyed Hollywood from head to toe twice looking for flaws. Amber smelled her favorite perfume she was wearing. "Tory Burch!"

"Just like heaven baby!" Hollywood voiced, as they high fived each other. "Thanks for coming down here," she walked on the opposite side of the bed. "I needed someone to keep me company. It's so lonely out here without Redline," she walked over to the window and stared down at the tiny cars zipping by.

"I feel you girl. He talks about you all the time. It feels like I already know you," Amber said truthfully, gazing at the many tubes going inside of Flagg's body.

Hollywood turned around facing her, "Really?! What does he say?" she asked as a smiled fluttered across her face.

"Girl, you know how nigga's are. Once the woman they love ain't around, that's when they start to open their eyes and realize what they really had," she winked her right eye. "He just always talks about how much he loves and misses you. And how much you mean to him and how he feels bad for leaving you out here alone."

Hollywood squeezed her eyelids shut trying to stop her tears before they raced down her cheeks. She wiped at the tears with the back of her hand.

"Amber you just don't know, I'll die for his red ass," she reached for a few tissues from the bedside table.

"I know the feeling. Trust me I do. Anyway, sorry to hear about your brother too. Have you heard anything about who did it?" Amber asked, pulling her luggage toward a chair in the corner of the room. She sat down and blew a breath of air out before taking off her high heels.

"N'all, the police said they'd call if they come across any leads. You know how that shit goes. But as long as I have breath in my body, I won't stop looking," Hollywood instantly transformed from a damsel in distress to Queen Latifah in Set it Off. "I'm gonna ride for my little brother. I don't give a fuck how long it takes. Just let me find out, and it's gonna be raining bullets in H-town for real," she paced the floor with her thoughts focused on payback.

"Just let me know what I can do to help. I'm down, Redline sent me down here to make sure you're ok. And that's what I'm gonna do. I also have this money for you too," Amber said, rubbing her feet together.

Eying Amber's perfectly pedicured toes, "Alright, I can use all the help I can get. Cause two bitches are way better than one," Hollywood stopped and stared down at Flagg. "Don't worry, I'm gonna find out who done this shit," she turned around and looked at Amber. "Did you book you a room yet? If not, you can stay with me."

"No, I haven't had a chance to do anything yet," she slipped her feet back into her heels.

"Well let's get out of here. We can come back another time. Because looking at Flagg and thinking about my brother, isn't making me feel any better," Hollywood rubbed Flagg's hand and her and Amber left the hospital.

Thoughts flooded across her mind heavily that even Noah's ark could've floated through. She kept a predominate attitude about vindicating her brother's death. And once she had her mind set on doing something, there was no turning back.

$$$

CHAPTER 14

"FLASHBACKS"
(GLASS HOUSE)

Redline stood in the long commissary line waiting to make every two weeks store purchases. Commissary was necessary. It made prison life more bearable for a lot of inmates. It also made it more dangerous and life threatening for the weaker ones. The hallway was hot and humid as the early morning sun pierced through the windowpanes. He stood at the back of the line contemplating about a conversation he had with his connect Himee...

"My friend, why you no get more. You get same number each time. You no like mucho dinero (a lot of money). Los mes agaras, lo mas dinero que ases" (the more you get the more money you make), Himee explained in Spanish adjusting his custom-made cowboy hat. "Me no have no problem with give you more amigo," he continued in broken English.

"Look out Himee, it pays not to be to be greedy in the game. The more work I get, the more people I have to fuck with. That's when the hating comes in," Redline expressed, looking around the big 100-acre ranch. Himee had his people walking around strapped ready for war if necessary. "If it ain't broke don't fix it. You feel me?" Redline looked at Himee and smiled.

"Me like it! Me like it! It no broke, no fix it," Himee laughed passing Redline an ice cold Modelo. "Me like you bidness amigo," he took a big drink of beer almost chugging the whole bottle in one gulp.

"AHHH! Mucho bueno, Mucho bueno, (very good, very good), they both shared a laugh and shook hand.

Redline smiled, nodding his head at the memory like it was just yesterday. The commissary line shortened a nice bit, but it was still long. Some inmates stood in line for at least an hour only to find out that they were broke. Redline glanced at several inmates as they walked by with their heads down headed back to the cellblock empty handed. Some of them had an image to uphold and returning to the cellblock without any commissary, after talking shit about how much money they had wasn't a good look. Redline had his back against the wall and slid down and sat on the floor. The temperature started to rise as the wind blew heat through the busted windows. He started thinking about Hollywood. His mind reversed back to the day, before they were intimate with each other for the first time...

Redline sat behind the wheel of his pearl white 1996 Chevy Impala. His car idled quietly. The air conditioner blew snowball cold. The twin exhaust pipes hummed, waiting to be heard. He was posted up on the corner of Beechnut and Wilcrest at a Valero gas station. There he impatiently waited while looking down at his cellphone for the tenth time. His eyes beamed in on everything that moved, even the trash blowing across the parking lot. He looked down at his cellphone than dialed a number. The line rang three times before it was answered.

"What's going on man?" Ant Frank answered, down shifting the big 18-wheeler due to traffic on the Beltway.

"Where you at pimp? I been posted up for ten minutes," Redline informed him with a frown on his face. Ant Frank was a bonafide hustler from his neighborhood Overbrook. They used to sell rocks together in 1991. Running up to cars with a hand full of stones is how they came up.

"I'm right here passing up Richmond. The Beltway is jammed packed. Plus, you know I'm rolling in this big ass truck nigga," Ant Frank explained, pulling down on the loud ass horn, as a no driving Mexican cut in front of him with no turn signal.

"I'll be pulling up in about five minutes," he gazed in his big side mirror before turning on his right signal light.

"Bet! Meet me at the Asian supermarket. I been posted up here too long," Redline placed his car into gear and eased out of the Valero parking lot.

"Alright!" Ant Frank ended the call turning up his thunderous sound system.

At the time, he'd been out of prison for 4 years. He was still working on his exit plan out of the game. He went to HCC (Houston Community College) and took up truck driving class. Once he received his CDL; he took his show on the road.

Redline parked his Impala facing Beechnut Street. That way he could see when Ant Frank pulled up, or anyone else. Hershylwood Hardheads vibed through the sound system. Lil' KeKe, Archie Lee, Duke, and Knocky expressed themselves how they hit the highway. Redline nodded his head to the self-relating lyric's as he waited. His cellphone rang through the stereo, "I'm here pimp," he answered, as his eyes locked in on the big candy red 18-wheeler chromed out with show lights all over. He popped open his trunk.

"Pulling up," Ant Frank said, turning the big candy red attraction on 18 wheels into the parking lot. He stopped once he blocked off Redlines car from the main intersection. He hopped out and opened the trailer door.

Redline was already walking up carrying a big blue ice cooler filled with 6 five-pound circles of solid cheese. Inside the middle of each one sat 1,008 grams of cocaine compressed.

"Same play Ant. Just bring me a hundred and fifty, whatever you make over is yours," Redline said, lifting the cooler onto the back of the trailer. "We good?"

"What's understood don't need to be explained. I'll hit you back in two or three days at the most," Ant climbed up onto the back of the trailer and took the cooler and unloaded it. He placed the cheese neatly with the rest of the dairy products. The back of the trailer was equipped with a refrigerated section. Ant secured the master lock into place. He slid the empty cooler towards the door of the trailer.

"Bet that! I'll catch you later," Redline grabbed the empty cooler and placed it back inside of the trunk. He surveyed his surroundings before getting back into his vehicle. He felt the earth quaking bass vibrating his whole car. Master P was pouring out of the cab of Ant's truck.

"FUCK THEM OTHER NIGGAS I'LL RIDE FOR MY NIGGAS WHAAAT! FUCK THEM OTHER NIGGAS I'LL DIE FOR MY NIGGAS WHAAAT!"

Redline shook his head as the hard-hitting deep bass shook the inside of his body. He put his car into gear and drove to the Gameroom on Beechnut. He knew Ant Frank was making a nice cut taxing his cliental in North Carolina. Redline was charging them $30,000 a book if they came to Houston. Ant Frank was popping their ass an extra $10,000, and they still blessed his game for delivering with no problems. He made over $50,000 easily. He took the same trip twice a month raking in the same amount or more.

The Gameroom was packed for a Thursday night. Redline couldn't find a parking spot so he maneuvered the white Impala slowly over the curb and parked a few feet away from the sidewalk, allowing enough space for pedestrians to walk through.

He dialed the familiar digits and the line rang, "I'm outside pimp. Y'all come at the same time," Redline gazed in all of his mirrors.

"Alright, here we come," Spud said ending the call. "Look out Jay! Redline outside come on," Spud told his partner in crime before downing the rest of the apple Cîroc he was drinking. Jay put down the pool stick and followed Spud outside.

The parking lot had a few slut buckets walking around trying their best to be noticed. Like their shorts between their pussy lips and butt cheeks wasn't enough. Spud and Jay saw Redline parked along the sidewalk with his park lights on.

"Man, that nigga Redline shit clean," Jay complimented, nodding his head looking at the pearl white Impala.

"That could be yo shit clean like that, if you stop tricking off yo breed on them mud ducks," Spud laughed, making his homeboy mad.

"Man fuck you! Hating ass nigga!" Jay snapped with an attitude. He knew Spud was right, but he wasn't trying to hear it.

Redline saw the two walking up and unlocked the doors. Spud got into the front and Jay sat in the backseat right behind him. "What's up hustla's?" Redline asked, as soon as both doors closed.

"Koolaiding, making this money," Spud said, reaching for the Phillie Southern Blend cigarillo packed with Gorilla Glue that was resting behind his ear.

"Same shit different smell," Jay acknowledged, leaning on the armrest.

"Y'all want another one," Redline asked, glancing at Spud firing up the cigarillo.

"Let me give you yo bread—for the first—one. I can't let you bury me in a hole," Spud said between hits. He passed the cigarillo to Redline and reached into his pocket and counted out the $7,000 he owed. Redline fronted him and Jay a brick for $20,000.

"I ain't ready, but here goes three thousand," Jay said passing Redline the wad of cash. "I owe you two thousand."

"If you leave them cum drunk bitches alone, you'll have some money," Spud said, making fun of his homeboy like always.

Jay pushed him in the back of his head, "Damn bitch ass nigga, you worse than Wendy Williams," he grabbed the cigarillo Redline passed to him and took a drag.

"So, you niggas want this last one or not?" Redline stressed, not really wanting to ride any further with it. He'd rather take his chances with his two hustlers than get pulled over by the law.

"Yeah!" Jay barked, before uncontrollably coughing up the potent smoke.

Redline gazed at him in the rearview mirror, "Make sure all your bread is straight next time. Ain't no reason for none of y'all to come up short, you feel me?" he kept his eyes glued on Jay before he popped open the trunk. "Get the grocery bag in the trunk."

Jay was the first one out of the car with a smile on his face.

"Make sure you keep him on top of his game Spud," Redline stressed, raising his eyebrows watching Jay close the trunk through the rearview mirror.

"We good man, I got him. Your girl up in there," Spud informed, detouring Redline's mind away from his homeboy Jay.

"Tell her to bring me a double shot of Silver Patron on the rocks," his eyes scanned the parking lot.

"Alright, I'll tell her. Good looking out Redline," Spud shook his hand firmly before going back inside the Gameroom.

$$$

Hollywood was at the pool table finishing off her third player. Shooting pool was her side hustle. Every man underestimated her capabilities when it came down to her pure natural skills. She was a born pool shark.

"Eightball side pocket," Hollywood called out, already adding the $500 to the $800 she had in her pocket for 15 minutes' worth of fun.

"I got a hundred you don't make it," Spud interrupted, slapping a $100 bill on the ledge of the pool table.

"I'm not even gonna do you like that lil' Spud," Hollywood said, focusing back on her winning shot. "Eightball side pocket," she said again looking at Spud shaking her head.

"Don't help me help the bear!" Spud capped back "Bet!"

"That's a bet to you lil' daddy," Hollywood shot back at him. "Some niggas never learn," she eyed the cue ball at the end of her stick.

She finessed the pool stick slowly between her thumb and index finger. Right when she was about to make direct contact with the cue ball...

"Redline said bring him a double shot of Silver Patron on the rocks," Spud laughed as Hollywood banked the Eightball off the side cushion. "I told you to help the bear," he said, holding out his palm.

"That was real nice. I should've known your ass was up to something," Hollywood watched as the dude she was playing drained two of the four balls he had remaining on the table. He drained one more ball in, but the cue ball followed right behind it.

"Eightball corner pocket," she looked at Spud. "Boy, you ain't no good," then lined up the cue ball and crashed the Eightball in the corner pocket with force.

Spud smiled as she collected her winnings. He still had his arm outstretched and palm open. Hollywood laughed and slapped a $100 bill in his hand before making her way towards the bar.

"Thanks, big sis!" Spud hollered out over the loud music.

Hollywood waved him off with her hand and kept walking towards the bar. She had on a pair of tight baby blue jeans with the Chanel logos all over them. She sported a thin white button up Chanel shirt with baby blue cuffs and collar. On her pretty feet was a pair of open-toed three-inch white Chanel heels. Her DD's were getting all of the attention with her first two top buttons undone.

The bar was packed with every seat filled with a body. People were standing all along the bar trying to get the bartenders attention, waving hands or even hollering out. Hollywood squeezed her soft nicely shaped frame between two dudes. They both looked down at her with frowns on their faces, until they saw how beautiful she was. That was when their frowns turned upside down instantly. Hollywood flagged down the bartender with a crisp Ben Frank.

"Hey! Let me get a double shot of Silver Patron on the rocks. And a strawberry kiwi Boosie Juice," Hollywood ordered, holding her hands together on the bar top. Her ears perked up when she heard two dudes on her left side talking.

"Say, they got this fool posted up outside like he own the joint. I saw lil' Jay get a grocery bag out of his trunk. And you know him, and the nigga Spud be getting the bread," Petey Gun said, finishing the rest of his watered-down Hennessey, then sparking up a Kool Filter King.

"What kind of car the nigga in?" Bird asked, nursing on his second glass of peach Amsterdam, thumping his Newport short ashes in an empty glass.

"A white Impala like DJ Screw," Petey Gun answered, with excitement in his voice. He inhaled his last hit on the cigarette down to the filter.

Hollywood's eyebrows raised and she became very attentive when she heard that. She watched the two dudes make their exit. Immediately she dialed Redline's phone to warn him of possible danger headed his way. The line went to voicemail.

$$$

Bird noticed the white Impala shining like a brand-new car. He peeped around the parking lot before pulling out a .9mm Mauser. He nodded his head at Petey Gun signaling for him to take the other side. This wasn't their first-time relieving niggas of their belongings, so they knew each other's role.

Redline glanced at his cellphone after watching two dudes walk out of the Gameroom. Hollywood called again. He looked back down at his phone. When he gazed back up the two dudes were gone. He peered down at his phone and noticed Hollywood calling again. A loud tapping on his passenger window made him jar his head up instantly. A dark figure held a gun pointed directly at his face. Redline's hand twitched as his mind contemplated on grabbing the blue steel .45 Magnum that sat between his legs.

As if reading his mind, "Don't even think about it nigga," Bird said, opening up the passenger door.

Redline was about to make his move despite the warning. A dark shadow appeared on his driver's side conceding the thought of reaching for his weapon. He stared down another barrel. The odds were not in his favor and dying over a car and some money wasn't worth it.

$$\$\$\$$

Hollywood dialed Redline's number three times. Her calls went to voicemail each time. She grabbed her drinks and told the bartender to keep the change. She navigated her way quickly through the crowded Gameroom towards the exit. Her eyes locked in on the dude that sat next to her at the bar. Instead of holding a drink in his hand, he held a big pistol pointed inside Redline's car. Hollywood dropped the drinks she had in her hands and reached inside her purse and grabbed ahold of a chrome .32 automatic.

$$\$\$\$$

"Don't try nothing fancy Al B Sure looking ass nigga. PG, get the nigga's gun," Bird ordered, right before a shot rang out, causing him to duck down. The next shot drilled into the back of his head dropping him in the parking lot.

Redline used the distraction to his advantage. He quickly opened his door and saw the other gunman ducked down at the rear of his car. The sudden gunfire startled him that he dropped his gun on the sidewalk. Redline couldn't believe his luck. He grabbed the fuck boy around his neck and squeezed with all his strength. The dude slapped at Redline's forearm trying to gasp for air. His body became limp under the death grip. Redline squeezed and squeezed, shaking him like a pit bulldog before letting him drop to the ground. Everything happened so fast he forgot about his .45 he had in the car.

"Bunny rabbit his pockets. Fuck these niggas," Hollywood barked, with the .32 still in her hand. She put the gun on the front seat and emptied the dead man's pockets, turning them inside out.

"Fuck that dumb shit, get in the car," Redline ordered in a demanding voice. "Get in the mutha fuckin car!" he yelled louder, snapping Hollywood out of her task. He looked around and saw people pouring out of the Gameroom gawking. "Get in the goddamn car Hollywood!" That got her full undivided attention. She hopped in the car and slammed the door. Redline snatched the car into gear and got the fuck out of Dodge.

"Don't be fuckin' yelling at me like you crazy. You act like I did something wrong instead of those two niggas," Hollywood placed her back against the door and continued barking. "Here I am out here risking my life for your shit colored ass. I'm not the one who had you looking down the barrel of death," she went on non-stop without Redline saying a single word. "I guess your ears are stopped up from me popping that nigga's top," she snapped, continuing to dig deeper underneath his skin.

Redline held his composure and kept his eyes darting to each mirror. He made sure that he maintained the speed limit. Getting pulled over for speeding wasn't a smart way to go out. Especially with two guns in the car, and one of them had a fresh body on it. Hollywood carried on expressing herself. He knew how she felt for him, so by her talking recklessly and out of the side of her neck, he overlooked it. He exited the Beltway and merged on 59 North headed towards 288 South. He gazed at Hollywood sitting in the same position with her arms folded across her chest defensively. Redline called Spud to see if he heard what happened.

"What's good big homie," Spud answered, watching as Jay broke down the book evenly.

"You hear about the shooting at the Gameroom," Redline wondered, signaling over to his left-hand lane.

"Yea, they said some fool in a white car aired that bitch out and killed two niggas," Spud relayed what he had heard from the streets. "I'm glad we left that bitch. After I told Hollywood what you said, me and Jay burned off."

"Alright! I was just trying to find out what was up. If you hear about anything else just let me know," Redline felt Hollywood's eyes peering upside his head.

"Will do," Spud ended the call.

Hollywood stared at Redline waiting for him to lace her up on what he heard. Her eyebrows were raised, and her facial expression said the rest. Redline looked at her and shook his head. That made her madder.

"So, you not gonna let me know what's up?"

"We good!" Redline said exiting Old Spanish Trail. He smiled when he heard her grunt loud. He made a left turn at the red light and crossed over 288 freeway. He made a left turn on Alleghany Street headed to The Golden Motel, his honeycomb hideout. He parked down the street next to Dreams lounge and turned the car off. He dialed a number on his cellphone which was answered on the first ring.

"Talk to me," Mike B answered, already knowing it was Redline.

"I need a one piece of burnt toast. The white ghost is on the corner of Dixie, down the street from Dreams. Break that strap down and make the parts disappear. The keys and your money is under the seat," Redline explained carefully, gazing around.

"I got you, later," Mike B ended the call, making a U-turn on Laport Road, heading towards the money.

"Here, go to the motel and get a room. Tell 'em you want room 25," Redline said handing her a $100 bill. He held the money in his hand until she snatched it away.

"So, I'm supposed to be a good little bitch and do what master says huh?" she took a deep breath then exhaled.

"Leave that gun in the car too."

"Yes sir!" she said smartly before getting out of the car. She closed the door and walked towards the motel.

Redline laughed to himself as he watched her strut down the street towards the motel. He smiled as the drivers stopped and blew their horns. They were trying to buy some pussy, and he knew Hollywood was serving them some very fine choice words. He tucked the .45 Magnum in his waistband then placed the money and Hollywood's gun underneath the front seat along with the car keys. Redline really didn't want to depart with his 1996 classic. He looked down at his black face Movado watch. He took one last look over the inside making sure he didn't leave anything before he got out. He peeped his surroundings casually then fired up his last Dutch Master cigarillo packed with Paris Og. He glanced once more at his car then made his wat to The Golden Motel, better known as his honeycomb hideout.

Hollywood was standing outside of the office when Redline walked up. "He gave me room 22. He said the toilet was broken in room 25," she explained, following behind him. She looked at room 22 as he walked by it. "I said room—!" she closed her mouth and followed his lead.

Redline stopped at room 25 which was located on the corner end of the motel. He unlocked the door and walked in. "Hey, lock the door and put the security bar behind it. And turn on the a/c," he said, grabbing the remote control bringing the flat screen on the wall to life. He sat the .45 on the bedside table and went into the bathroom and closed the door.

Hollywood looked around the room only to see her reflection staring back at her. Each wall was completely covered in mirrors, even the ceiling. A big 50-gallon fish tank shined brightly in the corner of the room capturing her attention. The fluorescent blue light glowed off the diamonds, gold, and platinum jewelry that covered the bottom of the fish tank. "Damn that's a lot of jewelry,' she said quietly. "Them some ugly ass fish!"

Redline stood underneath the steamy shower head. The massaging shower erased all problems from his mind. He lathered up from head to toe. His mind shot to Hollywood washing his back. "Hollywood!" he yelled out, picturing her ass naked rubbing on his body. "Hollywood!" he called out again sliding the shower curtain back listening to hear if she responded. When he didn't get a response back, he hurried out of the shower alarmed. He snatched open the door and saw Hollywood squatted down in front of the fish tank looking inside.

"You didn't hear me calling yo ass?" Redline asked, standing there butt naked with water dripping down his well-chiseled body.

"N'all, I was tripping on all this jewelry, and these ugly ass fish with big teeth," she said, licking her lips looking at his fat red dick hanging.

"You ain't got no eye control huh? I wanted you to come and wash my back," he knew what she was about to ask when she gazed back at the aquarium. "And yeah, everything except the diamonds," Redline turned around and walked back into the bathroom.

Hollywood removed her clothing piece by piece thinking what she was about to do. She looked at herself in the mirror. She was glad that she shaved all over when she took a shower this morning. She pushed open the door and the steam from the hot shower rushed out. She stepped into the shower not caring that her hair was about to get soaked. She grabbed the soap from the holder and took the towel out of his hand. Redline stood underneath the steady stream of water with both hands resting on the wall. Hollywood lathered up the towel with the bar of white Dove soap. She began to wash his back. Her juices began to flow as she felt his hard body. She watched as the soap ran down his butt. She rubbed his butt real good, washing him way down to his feet. Redline turned around.

"You like that?" Hollywood asked, not taking her eyes away from the hard-fat cock in front of her face.

"Yeah!" Redline said, as his dick throbbed up and down.

"I'm not talking to you. I'm talking to him," she pointed at the little man staring her down. She wrapped her full lips around the head of the penis and sucked slowly. She eased her way down at her own pace. As soon as he grabbed the back of her head she stopped. "I don't need no help I got this!"

"Alright damn, my bad," he placed his hand back on the wall and watched her go back to work.

Hollywood grabbed a hold of his dick and got back to her duty. She sucked on his manhood like she was teaching a lesson. She felt his dick jumping in her mouth. She continued to stroke his pole as she bobbed her head with the same motion. Redline started thrusting his hips matching her strokes. Hollywood felt his pipe expand in her mouth. She knew he was about to cum. "Here you go," she said, standing up handing him the soap and towel with a smile on her face.

"Turn around! Put your hands on the wall and spread 'em!" Redline ordered, applying soap to the towel with a smirk on his face. He watched lustfully as she obeyed his command.

"Yes, sir officer!" Hollywood responded, biting down on her bottom lip, placing her hands high on the tile and spreading her legs as wide as she could.

"You have the right to back your ass up. You have the right to grab your ankles if you please," he informed, washing her body with slow circular strokes. "You have the right to continue sucking my dick," that made her laugh. "You have the right to spread your ass cheeks," Redline stepped closer, allowing his acme brick hard on to slide between her butt cheeks.

Hollywood moaned out when she felt his thickness pass over her rectum and parked in between her butt cheeks. Redline made his dick jump. He grabbed it then slapped it against her fat soft bubble bottom. He kissed her behind the ear causing another moan to escape her mouth. He stepped away from the stream of water and watched as the soap ran down her perfect frame.

"Turn around!" he licked his lips at the wonderful site.

Hollywood looked down at his erection. She couldn't wait to feel his thickness penetrate her tight pussy. She stared at him as he bathed her body. Her nipples were so hard they protruded through the soap suds. He raised up one of her legs and rested it on the rim of the tub. He bathed her leg all the way down to the foot, then repeated the process on the other leg. He rubbed gently but thoroughly between her legs, making sure what he was about to eat was nice and clean. After rinsing her clean Redline kneeled and began sucking and kissing her pretty fat coochie. He locked his lips around her pearl tongue, sucking as his tongue worked vigorously. Hollywood grabbed the back of his head, something she didn't like at all. However, Redline didn't mind as he continued to devour his dish. Her moans of pleasure excited him as he spread her lips apart with one hand and jacked himself off with the other. Hollywood came in his mouth as he shot his load all over her foot. They washed their kids down the drain and took round two to the king size bed.

$$\$\$\$$$

"Look out man! Hey, your name Jones?" an inmate asked. "The commissary lady calling you," he said, walking away with a big fat sack of groceries.

"Alright! Good looking out," Redline was the only one left in the line. He got up trying to conceal the hard on he had.

He smiled at the memory. Him and Hollywood sexed each other in every position they could think of that day. He handed the commissary worker his slip.

"You didn't hear me calling you Jones?" Miss Lacy asked, looking at him waiting for an answer.

"I'm sorry Miss Lacy. I started thinking about the free world and zoned out," Redline answered honestly. He looked down making sure his semi hard on wasn't noticeable.

"N'all you good. I'm just ready to get the hell outta here," she said, scanning his purchases.

Redline sacked up all his stuff and headed back to the cell block. Once he got inside of his cell; he put up a sheet and masturbated looking at his pictures of Hollywood. After busting his nut, he put away his groceries and went to sleep. He dreamed of parole. He pictured his freedom. He had already dictated his own destiny.

$$\$\$\$$$

CHAPTER 15

"HOE CHECKING"
(KELLY COURT APARTMENTS)
HOUSTON, TEXAS

Fast Blacc was blowing through cash like he was a big-time celebrity. He spent over $150,000 on jewelry, and that was only for a bracelet and a necklace. TV Johnny gave him a deal he couldn't refuse, like always. His money started looking funny, so he went back to checking on his bitches.

Tiffany didn't have any plays to chunk his way. Little did he know, she was busting moves on her own. Ever since Fast Blacc played her out of $5,000, she kept all her licks to herself.

Mona hasn't brought anything to the table since the last incident with Peewee. However, she been texting him for a week trying to borrow money. Fast Blacc made a nice piece of change from their last lick. Between the money in the stash spot, and the currency he was paid to kill Peewee, that alone put him over $100,000. And like they say, fast money never last long.

Renee was from 5th Ward. A cute face, fat booty, busted and couldn't be trusted cum gussler. When it came down to making easy money, she had no respect or morals for the game. One day she got tired of her own kids and called Child Protection Services on herself. They took the kids away from her for being an unfit mother. And the sad part about that, the kids were happy to leave. Fast Blacc didn't give a damn about any of her scandalous ways, because he didn't trust her as far as he could see. He didn't eat, drink, or smoke anything she had. She was just a low down dirty rotten bitch, and maybe that's why they got along so good.

He always popped up without calling. That way she never had a chance to catch him slipping. He parked his car in front of the manager's office and walked to her apartment. Fast Blacc shook his head as he heard the loud music coming from inside of her apartment. He beat on the door so hard, the girl who stayed next door looked outside.

The music turned off. "Who the fuck is it? Beating on my muthin' fuckin' door like the law," Renee yelled, trying to peep through the peephole. "I ain't got time for no games," she was becoming irritated because she couldn't see who the fuck was at her door. Fast Blacc held his finger in front of the peephole. "Well yo stupid ass will be standing out there then," she hollered out, squinting her eye trying to see through the peephole standing on her tip toes.

"Girl open up the fuckin' door," Fast Blacc voiced, removing his index finger away from the peephole.

Renee opened up the door, "Boy, yo black ass better stop playing like that. I almost shot through this mutha fucka," she said, placing a hand on her hip and the other hand on the door frame. "You gotta stop popping up over here like this. I might have company up in here one day," Renee said, looking around to see who was standing outside being nosey like she normally did.

"If yo ass had company you wouldn't even opened the fuckin' door. So, miss a pimp with that bullshit. You wanna get high or not?" Fast Blacc questioned, already knowing her answer.

Renee stepped off to the side allowing him to enter. "You got some of that good gas?" she asked, closing the door and locking the dead bolt lock.

"Yea, it's louder than your mouth," he laughed, as she turned up her nose. "I got some Tony Montana too," Fast Blacc sat down on the sofa and pulled out a 3.5 of white, and a 3.5 of Paris OG Kush. "Here roll this shit up," he tossed the bag of kush on the table and a pack of Backwoods. He poured the 8 ball of cocaine on the table. He used an old business card that sat on the table to chop and line up the dope with.

Renee had her eyes glued to the white powder sitting on her table. She gutted the cigarillos with her orange and black checkerboard nails, dumping the tobacco in a piece of paper she tore out of a magazine.

"That look like that good right there," she stressed, referring to the powdery white substance that silently called her name.

She watched as Fast Blacc made four hefty lines disappear, two into each nostril. She finished twisting the first cigarillo and blazed it up. She inhaled deeply holding her breath. Her lungs weren't ready for the OG kush. She coughed uncontrollably until her eyes watered and tears streamed down her face. "Here!" she said lowly, as she caught her breath passing the cigarillo to Fast Blacc.

He sucked his teeth with a grin on his face. "I told yo ass it was some loud," he passed her the rolled up $50 bill and sat back on the couch and enjoyed the cocaine draining down the back of his throat.

He dragged a couple of times on the cigarillo then sat it in the ashtray. He reached behind his ear and grabbed the sherm that was whispering to him. He watched as Renee vacuumed up the good powder he bought from Tron. He sparked up the Klumanady and inhaled slowly, enjoying the sensation as it took control of his body.

"Nigga, don't get to trippin' up in here," Renee said, when she looked up and saw him smoking a wet daddy. She grabbed the gas out of the ashtray and lit it back up. She took a couple of small hits this time. She turned the music back on and pulled the coffee table away from the sofa. She kneeled between his legs while he was still smoking on the sherm and unbuckled his pants. His dick popped out ready for trouble. Renee began polishing his helmet as Future rapped about Purple Rain in the background.

Fast Blacc was feeling different sensations all at the same time. The cocaine had him floating. The Paris OG had him buzzing. The formaldehyde had his senses working overtime. And the way Renee was swallowing his piece, nothing on earth felt better. His mind drifted back to the day he met Renee in Galveston two years ago.

"Bitch my rent is due. I'm two months behind on my car note. My bad ass kids need school clothes. I sold what I had left on my Longstar card to buy this outfit, and to get my hair done," Renee's homegirl Shalaun vented, as they walked along the Seawall in Galveston, Texas.

They both sported two-piece string bikinis that left little to one's imagination. "I ain't going home until I find me a nigga that's willing to spend some cash," Shalaun stressed, passing the Russian Cream Backwood laced with Purple Punch Kush.

"You wanna see some ass, we wanna see some cash," Renee sang, puffing on the good Hydro.

"MAKE IT RAIN TRICK, MAKE MAKE RAIN TRICK!" they both sung out loud, then started laughing.

The Seawall was crowded with people of all sorts. The sun was shining, and the cool breeze blew in off the ocean. It was the fourth of July weekend. Hustlers and ballers from all over showed up to show out. Some grinded all year just to pull up in a slab on Super Pokers or chrome rims. Big money, expensive clothes, flashy jewelry. It was more of a fashion show, and to let those in the streets know that you're eating. However, there was also the jack boys and conniving bitches out to get theirs too. Like Renee and Shalaun.

"Look out lil' momma! Come sit that fat pretty ass on this cool leather," Fast Blacc hollered out the window of his 1977 baby blue Cadillac sitting on 24's. The diamonds in his mouth sparkled like the rainbow flakes on his car.

"Who you talking to?" Shalaun questioned, hoping it was her. Cause God knew how hungry she really was. She stopped and placed a hand on her hip.

"Both of y'all, if y'all game. I ain't doing no tripping. My money longer than I-10," Fast Blacc macked with the intent of getting them both into his ride. "I got some of this good gas too," he saw the look on their faces. That was when he reached across the long seat and opened the passenger door. They looked at each other and hopped in. That was when Fast Blacc found out Renee and Shalaun were from 5th ward also, and they danced at club Roxy, and they knew how to suck a mean dick...

Fast Blacc smiled at the memory as Renee stroked him until he shot his load deep down her throat. She continued sucking his cock until he made her stop. Renee was a true dick sucker by heart. She was the only bitch he knew who could suck dick from sunup to sundown and still want more. After she put his black inner tube on flat a couple more times, she told Fast Blacc about a baller she met at the club. He was all ears after that.

Making easy money was right up his alley. Especially when it came down to putting that tool to work. Renee put the play into motion, and the rest was history. Fast Blacc was back to balling again...temporarily.

$ $ $

CHAPTER 16

"WAITING FOR A COME UP"
(JACK'S PAINT & BODY SHOP)
HOUSTON, TEXAS

Mona sat behind her desk at work frustrated. Her mind was locked in on finding another come up...fast. The money she made from the last lick with Fast Blacc was long gone. Instead of using it wisely like she should've, she ran through it like Allyson Felix. Nobody came in for Jack's candy paint special, and that alone had Mona's panties in a bunch.

"How are you doing today?" Mona greeted a customer as he walked in and rested his elbows on the counter.

"I'm straight! Is Jack here?" he asked, looking through the plexiglass towards the back of the shop.

"Are you interested in our special candy paint deluxe?" Mona questioned, with her fingers crossed underneath the counter. "It comes—,"

"I already got it miss lady," the dude replied, cutting her off from finishing what she was about to say. "Came in five months ago," he explained, pointing outside to the sparkling clean candy red Escalade sitting high on 26" chrome rims. "Thanks for asking though," he said, walking into the back of the shop.

Mona slammed her hand down on the counter, "FUCK!" she said out loud. She sat back down at her desk and tapped her fingers over the desktop. "I already got it miss lady," she mimicked the dude who just walked into the back of the shop. Mona overheard them talking about a guy name Peewee. They said someone killed him and jacked him for his car. Jack was telling the other dude that Peewee had just got his ride sprayed candy red three weeks ago.

Right then an idea thumped her brain. She peered out the window and wrote down the license plate number of the Cadillac Escalade. Her fingers went to work on the computer that sat in front of her. She typed in the plate number, year make and model, and the rest was like taking candy from a baby. The date, amount paid, code and location of his stash spot was available. A smile buzzed across her face. All the cars that Jack painted and worked on were right at the tip of her fingers. A few more licks like the last one and Mona was through. She toyed with the necklace Fast Blacc gave her. Selling it crossed her mind plenty of times. But for some strange reason, she couldn't depart with it.

Jack was getting on her nerves more and more each day. Ever since Mona jacked him off for $200, he couldn't keep his hands off her. She wanted to quit and go back to boosting. The thought wrestled with her conscious daily, but she needed the money, and going back to jail for stealing clothes wasn't her hustle anymore. Mona was a silver back gorilla when it came down to stealing clothes. She used to have a special made shopping bag with the inside lined with aluminum foil. That way the sensors wouldn't go off when she passed through the detectors on her way out the doors. Her mind slipped back to the day she was almost caught. Her special made shopping bag wasn't so special this particular day...

Mona was at Almeda Mall tearing Foley's and Dillard's a new asshole. She went through Dillard's and stole Polo shirts, jeans, shoes, socks, and underwear. She filled her bag to the max and made a trip to her car. She returned and went Levi, Chanel, and Dolce Gabbana shopping. She made two more trips to her Toyota Camry before going inside of Foley's and loading up. She was about to make her first trip to unload her goods and come back for more. Right when she passed through the sensor detectors they began to snitch. The alarm went off notifying everyone in hearing distance.

"Hey, you!" a security guard yelled out, pointing his finger at Mona.

That was all Mona needed to hear. She tucked the shopping bag under her arm and hauled ass. The security guard gave chase. He was keeping up until Mona turned it up a notch.

"Stop, Stop!" he gasped out, still running behind her.

Mona faked like she was about to cut left, but she shot off to the right. That was when the security guard's chase came to an end. He twisted his ankle and crashed down to the pavement. Mona gazed back and laughed. She ran across the street and dipped inside of a Fiesta supermarket. She sat inside the photo picture booth and closed the black curtain. She sat her bag down and the first person she called was Flagg. His line rang a few times and went to voicemail. She tried again and again, no luck.

"Damn it!" she said out loud, thinking who she could call next. Right when she was about to call her brother, her phone rang. "Hello," she answered hurriedly.

"What's up girl?" Flagg asked.

"I need you to come and get me now. The security at Almeda just got through chasing me. I left my car in the parking lot," Mona explained, almost out of breath.

"Where you at?" Flagg asked, turning down the radio in his car.

"I'm at the Fiesta across the freeway," Mona peeped through the hole in the black curtain.

"I'll be there in ten minutes, chill," Flagg ended the call.

True to his word, Flagg pulled up under 10 minutes. He called Mona and she came out. They left her car and came back to get it several hours later...

Mona couldn't stop smiling. She was still in love with Flagg after all these years. She wrote down the code and details of how to get into the Escalade's secret compartment. She picked up her phone and called Flagg. It went to voicemail like always. However, this time instead of hanging up, she left a message. "Hey Boo! I miss you. Call me whenever you can, bye," Mona ended the call, not knowing Flagg was laid up in Ben Taub Hospital fighting for his life.

CHAPTER 17

"PENITENTIARY CHANCES"
(GREYHOUND BUS STATION)
DOWNTOWN HOUSTON, TEXAS

The Greyhound Bus Station on South Main was alive with activity of all sorts. Individuals roamed the sidewalks with their minds on different missions. Dope seller's, drug addicts, Con men and women. The homeless stood on each corner panhandling, hoping they'd scrape up enough change to buy a few item's off the dollar menu from Mc Donald's across the street. And all of this took place under the watchful eye of Houston Police Officer's. As long no one was robbing killing and stealing, or causing a major disturbance, they paid them no attention.

Tron sat in a red hard plastic chair waiting for his bus departure to be announced over the loudspeaker. A burgundy Michael Kors backpack sat on the floor between his feet. Inside of the bag were 6 compressed kilos of cocaine, each stamped with a clover leaf, along with other items needed for his trip. He watched as people scurried towards their destination.

"Bus 12 to Atlanta now loading. Departure time, 15 minutes," a lady announced in an annoying voice over the intercom.

Tron gazed around cautiously before picking up his backpack. He proceeded straight to the bus without any hesitation. He handed the bus driver his ticket. The bus driver scanned his ticket then looked up into his eyes. Tron shifted the bag away from the driver's reach.

"I see you're headed to ATL huh son," the bus driver commented, handing back his ticket stub. "I heard they have a lot of big booty, fiiine women up there," he stressed, rubbing a hand across his uneven mustache as he chuckled.

"Yea chocolate city," Tron replied, grabbing his stub quickly walking up the steps. He didn't want to be rude by ignoring the old man. That would've only made the old timer pay closer attention to him.

Tron looked around until his eyes registered on the perfect seat. He placed his burgundy bag on the seat closest to the window and sat down. The restroom was on his right side in full peripheral view. That way he could see anyone entering or exiting the restroom without turning his head to look. His eyes took inventory of everything and everyone around him. He reclined his seat back and settled in, waiting for the other passengers to simmer down before he went to work. The bus driver strapped on his seatbelt, adjusted his Greyhound hat, and shifted the big vehicle into gear.

Tron watched as people shuffled in and out of the restroom early, which was a good thing. That way when it was time for him to handle his business, hopefully he wouldn't get disturbed. He watched as pedestrians moved throughout the crowded sidewalks with ease. The Greyhound bus reflected off each window as it passed by. Tron purposely stretched his arms turning his head to peep who was sitting behind him. Relaxing back in his seat he began thinking about what needed to be done. The last trip he took to Atlanta snatched his thoughts and trampled on his brain...

Tron had his backpack sitting on the floor of the bus. The bus driver made an unexpected stop that wasn't on the route. Tron sat straight up in his seat staring out the window. Three state trooper cars blocked off the bus. His eyes beamed in on the bold letters painted on the back which read K9 UNIT. Two troopers boarded the bus immediately along with their four-legged companions. Tron's heart was beating rapidly as he tried his best to remain calm.

"Everyone, please remain calm, and please remain seated. We'll be out of here before you know it," one of the troopers announced loud and clear. "No one make any sudden moves, please!" the canine led the way towards the back of the bus.

"Come on girl!" the last trooper said to his dog that was sniffing around Tron's seat. He pulled the dog's leash and they walked away. The canine looked directly back at him. It felt like the dog was giving him a warning. That made Tron's flesh crawl. His heart rate settled down as he watched the troopers load their dogs back into the car...

That was one day and one close call Tron would never forget. He glanced around and noticed everyone was kicked back and comfortable. He picked up his bag and walked into the restroom. He locked the door behind him then sat his backpack on the counter. He quickly went to work. He unzipped his bag and removed the bricks of cocaine. He took out two 10-pound plastic weights and sat them on the floor along with 4 waterproof Ziploc bags. He worked his arm inside of a shoulder length rubber glove. Each book of cocaine was sealed in an airtight wrapping. He placed 3 kilos in one Ziploc bag and sealed it up. After checking the bag carefully making sure it was sealed, he placed it inside of another Ziploc bag along with a 10-pound weight.

He repeated the same technique with the next 3 bricks of powder. Once he finished, Tron carefully placed them down in the commode. The dark blue water camouflaged the packages at the bottom of the stainless-steel toilet. He removed the glove, rolled it up and tossed it out the air chute.

Next, he scattered paper towels all over the floor to make the restroom appear nasty and dirtier than it already was. Tron dropped paper towels in the toilet to help conceal what rested at the bottom. He took a second look over everything, nodding his head up and down then returned to his seat.

The passengers were basically in the same positions they were when he left. He placed his bag in the empty seat across from him. Tron glanced down at his Bulova timepiece and reclined his seat back once again. It was a long 12-hour trip to Atlanta, but it was well worth it. He pondered on the seed of greed he planted, which sprouted within a couple of days. It was only a matter of time before his money tree begin to produce. The ball was in his hand and time was on his side. He called Lil' Reggie informing him of his estimated time of arrival. Tron had known Lil' Reggie for years, well before he blew up and became a major record label owner, and a household name. He wondered why Lil' Reggie was still fiddling around in the dope game when he was already well established.

Then Tron asked himself that same question. Only to be answered with another thought initially ignoring the truth that he was addicted to the streets. His mind bounced to how Ralo was recklessly making irrational decisions. He shook his head at the thought. All it took was one stew head to ruin a multimillion-dollar plan. And before Tron allowed that to happen, someone was going to be found dead and stinking.

A few more thoughts danced around his mind and before he knew it, it was time to change buses. Tron quickly handled the task at hand before the bus came to a complete stop. He was in and out of the restroom with no delay. He slid both arms through the straps of his Michael Kors backpack and exited the bus.

The second bus to ATL was waiting at the station. He boarded and was lucky to find an empty seat welcoming him at the back of the bus. He removed the bag from his back and sat it on the seat next to him by the window. He peered casually at the riders who were already seated. Some were sleeping or resting their eyes, as other's murmured amongst each other watching who got onto the bus.

The driver of the transportation vehicle allowed riders 10 minutes to enter before he closed the doors. He finessed the big bus skillfully through midday traffic merging onto the highway. Tron melted back into his seat and patiently waited 30 minutes into the ride. Quick and discreet. He stepped into the restroom and duplicated the procedure.

He glanced up at the mirror as he washed his hands. His reflection stared back shaking his head. No one knew about his elbow deep in shit trips. It wasn't like he gave a damn, but certain tricks were meant to be kept a secret. He dried his hands, grabbed his bag and returned to his seat. Tron peeped at his watch and closed his eyelids for the remaining three and a half hours.

$$$

CHAPTER 18

"BACK TO BUSINESS"
(TOP'S STRIP CLUB)
KILLEEN, TEXAS

L il' Brandon stood in his office overlooking his establishment.
Him and his girl KeKe invested their money into the strip
club. Going against her better judgement of saying no, KeKe
gave in and drained her savings account. She wanted to stand by her
man and let him lead the way. However, they came to a mutual agreement with each other. That if the club didn't make at least half of their
money back in the first year, they agreed to shut it down. Also, if they
didn't make 50% profit by the time she graduated from college, they
were selling it. Her Bachelor's degree in Business took four years.
KeKe felt like that was more than enough time to have doubled their
money, if not more.

Lil' Brandon eyes cast through the two-way mirror behind the bar.
It was an ok crowd for a Tuesday night. He charged $10 at the door
and $20 on weekends. The girls he hired was how he raked in most of
his profit. Over half of them solicited their bodies. His first question
upon hiring was, do you sell pussy? So, since he was willing to allow
them to use his place of business for illegal activities, he charged $100
each time one of the girls entered one of the 4 VIP rooms. Lil'
Brandon installed a camera at the end of each hallway. That way he
wouldn't miss out on any money. His mind was programed not to trust
a pussy seller.

He peered at the ladies getting their money. Dancing on stage, giving lap dances, flirting heavily at the bar in order to get customer's and free drinks. Lil' Brandon nodded his head slowly up and down. He had about 6 months until KeKe reeled in her degree. He made well over the $70,000 they invested almost four years ago. He knew it was time to change lanes before lady luck ran out.

He also wanted to use the $150,000 profit to pay off their cars and buy them a house. He was going to give the $70,000 they started off with to KeKe. That way she could start her real-estate business. They say every thug has a lady he's weak behind. Lil' Brandon thought back to how he met KeKe...

Club Oasis was located on the Southwest side of Houston. A well-known party spot for those looking to enjoy themselves. Lil' Brandon stood with his back against the wall sipping on his second glass of Bumpy Face gin. His eyes were locked on a beautiful fine caramel colored female. He patrolled her every move, waiting for the right time to approach her. He watched as she turned down at least five dudes who tried to holler at her.

He gazed down at his unit. A fresh pair of gray and black suede Bo Jackson's on his feet. A clean pair of jet-black Levi's, and a Dolce and Gabbana short sleeve button up shirt, with a king of club on the front. Everything on his body was fresh, even his haircut. Lil' Brandon swallowed the corner of gin in his glass while his eyes stayed on his prize. He saw her walk away from her homegirls headed towards the dance floor. That was when he made his move. The closer he got to her the more attractive she became. She swayed her body to the sounds of Crime Mobb as she rocked her hips.

"Girl you move like my grandma," Lil' Brandon said, loud enough to capture her attention. "And you hard of hearing like her too," he stepped closer and saw her sparkling white teeth and pretty smile.

"No, you didn't! Boy you moving like a broke down mule," she shot back with a smile on her face. They both laughed.

"What's your name beautiful?" Lil' Brandon asked, looking at how her body was nicely shaped in the black tight deep V neck dress she was wearing.

"KeKe! What's your name?" she asked, peeping him from head to toe. KeKe took a quick mental note on how good he looked and smelled, and how his dress code was nice. She was feeling him already, and she didn't even know his name.

"Lil' Brandon. I like that dress you got on. Baby you killing it," he complimented, instantly causing another smile to appear on her face.

"You looking real nice yourself," KeKe said, taking a step closer in his space. "You here by yourself?" she wondered, moving her hips side to side.

"Yea! How about you?" already knowing the answer she was about to say.

"N'all, I'm here with my homegirl and my cousins," she smelled the fragrance coming from his body. "What kind of cologne is that?" she asked, taking another step closer to him.

"Polo Blue! You like it?" he smiled, as she nodded her head up and down indicating yes. "You wanna get something to drink?"

Before KeKe even had a chance to answer, "Girl, you need to let us know next time you decide to up and disappear," Shawanna said with a feisty attitude, turning up her nose as she scanned Lil' Brandon from head to toe.

"Yea girl! You had us looking for your ass, and you out here dancing with who knows," Stacey snapped, with her hands on her wide hips.

"Ain't that the truth," Red added her half cent in.

"Yea, yea, yea!" I know Lil' Brandon from school for y'all information. Brandon this is Stacey, Red, and Shawanna," KeKe introduced the trio as she pointed with her index finger. "Anyway, we about to head to the bar. Catch y'all later!" KeKe put her arm around Lil' Brandon's waist and they went to get their drink on...

That was the beginning of their 12-year relationship. Lil' Brandon scanned his eyes over the club once again. He stepped to the mini bar and poured himself a stout glass of Hennessy. He sat down and rested his legs up on the desktop. He took a sip of his drink and thought about his girl. He also contemplated on the dumb ass shit he was doing to make extra cash. He had a legal money-making business, but he still found himself backsliding into illegal activities.

It was only inevitable he would get shut down for prostitution eventually. That's why he decided to tell KeKe he was selling the club. And after the deal was finalized, he was going all the way legit. He sipped on his drink smiling at the thought.

$$$

CHAPTER 19

"A FUNNY FEELING"
(GREYHOUND BUS STATION)
ATLANTA, GEORGIA

Tron opened his eyelids. He beamed down at his watch and
noticed he'd been asleep for 3 hours. A feeling of being
watched circulated over his body. He darted his eyes
throughout the bus. No one was paying him any attention. He reached
for his cellphone and dialed Lil' Reggie's number.

The line rang a few times before it was answered, "What's the
word!" Lil' Reggie voiced.

"Same ole shit. I'll be pulling up in twenty minutes. Are you ready?"
Tron asked, watching as an old lady walked into the restroom.

"Yea, I got the traveler's check this morning."

"Cool, I'll hit you up again in a few," Tron said, rubbing the bridge
of his nose.

"Later!" Lil' Reggie ended the call.

Tron peered down at his timepiece again then gazed at the
restroom door. He couldn't shake the strange sensation that he was
being patrolled. He never ignored his inner feelings, so he stayed alert.

The old woman finally came out of the restroom. The smell stam-
peded out of the door. Tron turned up his nose. He waited until the
old lady sat back down in her seat. He grabbed his backpack and
walked into the restroom. He held open the air chute before going to
work, allowing some of the smell to be sucked out.

"Damn Grandma!" he said, shaking his head at the big ass turd floating in the toilet.

He pulled on his gloves, held his breath, and handled his business. After removing both packages from the toilet, he took them out of the first Ziploc bag which contained the 10-pound weights. Following his gut feeling, Tron changed up his routine. He put the weights in his backpack. He scooped up all the trash and put it in the trash can. He grabbed the bag, tied it up, and took it with him. The bus was just turning into the station when he came out of the restroom. He eased back into his seat and sat the trash bag and backpack next to him.

"Now arriving in Atlanta! Please be sure to gather all of your belongings before you exit. All luggage below will be at baggage claim. Thank you for choosing and riding Greyhound," the male driver informed everyone over the bus loudspeaker as the big vehicle came to a stop.

Tron moved his eyes in every direction watching for anyone watching him. He looked out the windows on both sides for anything suspicious. The uncomfortable feeling stuck to him like gum on the ground. He hoisted his backpack on and picked up the trash bag. He stepped off the bus into the cool late-night Atlanta weather. Tron moved with means of a man on a money-making mission. He threw the plastic bag in the nearest trashcan and called Lil' Reggie.

"What's good," Lil' Reggie answered, exhaling his lungs that was filled with Moon Rock.

"Where you at?" Tron asked, walking towards the front of the bus station. People were out and about like it was 2 o'clock in the afternoon, instead of 2 o'clock in the morning.

"Looking at you like the law nigga," Lil' Reggie flicked his headlights on from the parking lot across the street.

Tron pressed the end button on his cellphone and cautiously made his way across the street. He glanced back to see if someone was following him. A sense of danger blew by causing a slight chill over his body. He shrugged it off and headed straight to Lil' Reggie's burnt orange Range Rover sitting on sparkling 26" chrome rims. The closer he approached the SUV, the heavier the odd feeling weighed upon him.

The moon was full illuminating brightly over the parking lot. Tron looked at the smoke rising out of the driver's side window. The windows were tinted dark obstructing any outside view. The feeling of being stalked tapped him on the shoulder causing him to stop and look around. He felt something was wrong, but he couldn't figure it out. He took a few more paces then opened up the front passenger's door.

"What's up nigga, you alright?" Lil' Reggie asked as soon as Tron got into the front seat.

"Yea I'm good. Just been having a funny feeling before I got off the bus," Tron explained, removing the backpack. "You got the traveler's check?" he looked at Lil" Reggie awaiting an answer, sitting the back-pack on the floor.

"You know I stay on point man," he passed Tron the check inside of one of his company's envelopes.

"I know, but business is business. You feel me?'" Tron enlightened, grabbing the envelope peeping the amount printed on the check.

"You ready to go fuck with some of these big booty bitches!?" Lil' Reggie asked, placing the SUV into gear.

"N'all, I think I'm gonna chill this time," Tron declined the offer. "I'm gonna head out early. Shit just don't-!" Three unmarked police cars whipped into the parking lot cutting his words off before he finished.

"FUCK!" Lil' Reggie shouted out, pounding on the steering wheel. He slammed on the brakes and put the SUV in park.

The unmarked police vehicles boxed the SUV in the parking lot. Red and blue lights flashed brightly from the grill and dashboard of each car. Six uncover officers aimed weapons at the Range Rover. Each face was etched with a square business demeanor look.

"You got anything on you?" Tron asked calmly, staring at the laws from behind the tinted windows.

"Yea! You mutha fucka!" Lil' Reggie barked, slamming his hand down on the steering wheel again.

Both doors were snatched open on the Range Rover at the same time. Two officers were on each side, and the other two covered the front. Tron and Lil Reggie were pulled out with such force they almost caught whiplash. They were separated from each other, but an officer had each of their face plastered on the hood of a hot car. Handcuffs were slapped on their wrist tightly.

"Man, what the fuck is wrong with you hoes," Lil' Reggie growled out, as one officer pressed his face down on the hood of the car, and another kicked his legs apart. "Do you hoes know who the fuck I am," he hollered to no avail.

"Shut your bitch ass up. We don't give a fuck about you, or how much money you got. Your bitch ass is going down tonight," one detective said, thoroughly searching Lil' Reggie and placing him in the backseat of the unmarked car.

Less than 20 feet away. Tron was being introduced to the same type of police brutality, Atlanta style. Detective Tubbs was assigned to bring down Lil' Reggie, but for some strange reason he had a hard on for Tron.

"You thought your slick ass was gonna skate back up outta here huh? Been watching you for a minute boy. And I must say, your very smooth. I would say smart, but your dumb ass didn't know when to stop," Detective Tubbs announced proudly, like he really did his homework.

"I don't know what the fuck you talking about," Tron said arrogantly, tightening up his muscles for the expected blow that never came.

"Yea, I know! All you punk mutha fuckas say the same shit when y'all get caught. I don't know what you talking about," Detective Tubbs mimicked in a whining voice.

He scanned over everything that was confiscated. "Put his ass in the car Joe," he said to his partner. He looked at Lil' Reggie who was sitting in the backseat of another unmarked vehicle.

"Hey Ward! What is he talking about?"

"Nothing, he's playing the big baller role," Detective Ward hollered back slamming the door shut.

Detective Tubbs walked over to the Range Rover and grabbed the burgundy backpack Tron had on. Him and his partner Joe had been waiting for this day. It's been over a year since they've started watching and waiting for the right time to bust Lil' Reggie's ass. Tron was just a bonus, or a drug smuggling piece of shit that Tubbs wanted off the streets.

Lil' Reggie stared at Tron from the backseat of the car he was in. He was wondering why the fuck Tron was smiling like this situation was a joke. Had Tron set him up after all these years of doing business. Lil' Reggie didn't put nothing past anyone, let alone a hustler from another state. Tron gazed at Lil' Reggie then winked his eye, as his smile widen. That made Lil' Reggie even more furious. He watched as the detective walked back to the car Tron was in, holding the backpack filled with dope. He knew he was about to go to jail. The detective threw the bag on the hood. Lil' Reggie cursed himself for being so stupid.

Tubbs was the lead detective in the case. Lil' Reggie and his crew had been on Atlanta's police departments radar for several years. They had their hands in just about every illegal activity there was. However, Tubbs was a firm believer that even a train could catch a flat.

"Joe, bring his ass here. I wanna see what he has to say about this," Tubbs said, patting on the Michael Kors bag. He watched as his partner roughly pulled Tron out of the car.

"What your punk ass got to say about this," Tubbs waved his hand over the backpack.

"You already know what he's going to say partner. That ain't mine. I don't know where you got that from," Joe imitated one of the numerous people they've arrested over the years who all said the same line. "Ain't that right?" Joe shoved Tron in the back trying to provoke him into resisting.

"What do you have to say boy?" Tubbs inquired, unzipping the backpack. "I guess this ain't your bag you had on your back when you came across the street...he looked in Tron's eyes. He raised the bag up to dump the contents out on the hood of the patrol car.

"Yea its mine! Been having it for almost a year. You like it?" Tron asked smartly, with a grin on his face. He watched as their facial expressions changed dramatically, when the two 10-pound weights dropped out of the bag denting the hood.

"What the fuck!" Joe blurted out, as his face cringed up as if he swallowed a rotten lemon.

He glimpsed up at his partner and recognized a look he'd known quite well. Flushed with anger. But to Joe's surprise, Tubbs didn't react the way he normally did. Instead of losing his temper he remained cool, calm, and copasetic. Detective Tubbs took a deep breath then blew air out through his lips. He ran a hand over his face. He rubbed on his chin lost in thought. He gazed at his other colleague shaking his head side to side. He knew this was their best if only opportunity to bring down Lil' Reggie and his drug smuggling associates.

Tubbs went back to search the Range Rover; a vehicle he'd wish he could afford. He rubbed his hands over every panel and each crevice applying pressure in search of a secret compartment. After a good 10 minutes of probing throughout the SUV he gave up.

"Joe, uncuff him," Tubbs announced defeated.

"What are you talking about? We can at least get their ass on tax evasion," Joe informed, looking at his partner. "This traveler's check is close to two hundred thousand dollars," he explained, handing Tubbs the check.

"I know how you feel Joe. Trust me, I feel the same way if not worse. Lil' Reggie has a multi-million-dollar company. This is chump change for him, it won't hold up in court," Tubbs looked at Tron and tore up the check into several pieces, stuffing them into his pocket. Tron smiled at the anger plastered all over his face.

Tubbs wanted to slap the smile completely off Tron's face. He casted his eyes around the parking lot and noticed a crowd had started to gather being nosey. "Hold his ass for a minute Joe. I'll be right back," Tubbs said, peering across the street at the bus station.

The smile Tron wore on his face slowly evaporated as he watched the detective walk across the street headed towards the bus station. He began to fidget and felt the grip of Tubbs partner tighten up on his arm. He looked around and saw the other undercover's gathered conversating facing the bus station. Tron peeked at Lil' Reggie who was watching his every move. His chin dropped down to his chest as he shook his head. A queasy feeling began to travel throughout his stomach causing his mouth to water. He spit on the ground and rocked side to side on his feet. He thought about how much effort he put forth into plotting and scheming a well put together plan, all for it to go to waste over 6 books of cocaine.

Tron raised his head up and saw the 6-foot-tall muscular built black detective walking back across the street empty handed. The big Kool Aid smile reappeared on his face. The closer the detective came into view, the angrier he looked. He walked up to the other detective's and said a few words. One of them opened up the back door to the car and released Lil' Reggie. He took the handcuffs off and handed him his belongings.

"Let him go Joe," Tubbs said, walking up to the car.

"You got away this time. But you can best believe next time I catch yo ass, you're going down," Tubbs slapped all of Tron's property off of the hood of the car onto the ground. Him and his partner got back into their unmarked car and backed away slowly. The other two cars followed behind them.

Tron bent over and picked up his stuff. He left the two 10-pound weights on the ground and grabbed his backpack. His mind was already made up. He wasn't coming back to Atlanta ever again. The profit was good, but this was one penitentiary chance he wasn't taking anymore.

Lil' Reggie sat behind the steering wheel of his SUV. He was watching and wondering what Tron had up his sleeves. Usually whenever they hooked up Tron would've had the work already with him. This time his backpack was empty, and that raised suspicion in Lil' Reggie's mind.

Tron opened the front door and hopped in, "Man let's get the fuck outta here," he threw his bag on the floor and shut the door. He looked over at Lil' Reggie and noticed the scowl expression on his face. "What's up with you man?" Tron questioned wearing a frown of his own.

"Nigga. what kind of games you playing man? First the laws show up! Then you came way down here with no dope," Lil' Reggie vented. gripping the steering wheel with his left hand. He began to get more heated when he saw the smile Tron had on his face.

"We been doing business to long man. I thought you knew me better than that. I don't know shit about the laws. I think they following yo ass. I got the books let's just get outta here," Tron voiced, buckling up his seatbelt.

"What!" he looked at him dumbfounded.

"Let's roll man, Fuck! I got you," Tron said, lowering his seat back relaxing. He felt Lil' Reggie's eyes boring into him.

Tron explained everything as they drove to his place of business. Lil' Reggie shook his head with a smile on his face listening as Tron laced him up. He felt better knowing that Tron didn't have any hidden agendas up his sleeves. He fired up a blunt and passed it to his right. Tron exhaled sharply.

The good hydro attacked his lungs causing him to cough. Seconds later his mind escaped reality. He pulled a few more times and passed the blunt back. Tron gazed out the window watching Atlanta's scenery pass by. He wasn't going to tell Lil' Reggie this was his last trip. He didn't feel like hearing any persuasive conversation.

Lil' Reggie pulled into the parking lot of his self-made enterprise. He informed his secretary on the way there, that he needed another traveler's check and a first-class plane ticket to Killeen, Texas. They cooled out for a few hours before heading back to the bus station. Tron advised Lil' Reggie to change vehicles. The Range Rover was way too easy to recognize. It attracted to much attention, and Tron wasn't trying to get stopped by the laws again.

They parked a block away from the bus station. Tron looked around before getting out of the car. He quickly made his way to the trash bin and recovered the dope. He hurried up the sidewalk and got back into the car. He handed Lil' Reggie the bag. Once he peeked inside a smile sneaked across his face.

"Let's get outta here!" Tron said, buckling up his seatbelt. "I can't even lie man. I thought you had some slick shit going on. When I saw that law dump that bag out, and no dope fell out. I just knew you was on some shady shit," Lil' Reggie admitted, putting the car into gear.

"I told you I was having a funny feeling. And when shit don't seem right with me, I get paranoid," Tron told him, glancing in his side mirror.

"Nigga I'm glad you was on note," Lil' Reggie replied, heading to the airport. "Square business I am."

Tron remained quiet the rest of the trip. His mind was on the unfinished task he had back in Texas. He had to make sure his plan went through. He dropped $5,000 to a well-known lawyer in Houston. She guaranteed him the outcome he was expecting or his money back. He thought about the time, money, and motivation put forth into his plan.

"It takes money to make money," Tron mumbled to himself, deep in thought.

"What you say nigga," Lil' Reggie asked, turning into the airport. He glanced at Tron.

"Nothing man, just thinking out loud," Tron grabbed his backpack off the backseat. "Thanks for looking out," he said, reaching for the door handle.

"Nigga, you the one who looked out for me. I need to be thanking yo ass," Lil' Reggie said, slowing the car to a stop where the signs read, pick up and drop off only.

"It ain't nothing, be safe nigga," Tron replied, before getting out of the car. He closed the door and watched Lil' Reggie drive away. He pulled out his cellphone and removed the sim card. Tron dropped the phone on the ground and stomped it to pieces. Once he was satisfied with his footwork, he went inside to board his flight.

$$$

CHAPTER 20

"UNEXPECTED VISITOR"
(BEN TAUB HOSPITAL)
HOUSTON, TEXAS

Hollywood lounged around her house sipping on her second glass of Stella Rosa Green Apple. She had just finished preparing grilled Hasselback chicken with cube roasted sweet potatoes. She was so used to cooking for Redline and herself there was always extra. And since Amber was visiting, there was enough for them both. She noticed the change in her weight and appetite. Her sleeping pattern was off also. She had trouble sleeping without waking up at different times of the night thinking about her brother's death. Having Amber around to vibe with helped her mind relax a lot.

Amber was the only person to step foot in their home since Redline went to prison several years ago. Hollywood knew the pangs of grief didn't last forever, and by isolating herself from others wouldn't make her situation any better.

Hollywood ate a small portion of food. She then fixed Amber's plate and placed it in the microwave before doing the dishes. She told Redline she'd go back to the hospital to find out if anything changed with Flagg's condition. She'd wished for Redline's freedom many of times, even before her brother was brutally killed. She needed him the way a fish needed water. She knew two people were better than one... because if one of them fell, the other could help their partner up. And

Hollywood needed a major boost to get herself back on track. She pranced in front of the mirror for about 15 minutes then placed her feet into a pair of Red Bottom heels and headed out the door.

Outside, Hollywood gazed around her neighborhood and reflected on the years they'd been staying there. She looked back at the beautiful 5-bedroom brick home. She smiled and got into her Lexus SUV and backed up out of the driveway. The Bluetooth on her cellphone automatically connected to the Pioneer system. She selected Yo Gotti from Da Piff's mixtapes and crafted her way through traffic. Different thoughts about her brother Peewee tinkered with her understanding.

Who would've wanted to kill her brother? Who knew about it, and just wasn't saying anything? She planned on getting his body cremated since over half of his face was missing. Hollywood shrugged her shoulders at the memory. She powered all four windows down, opened the sunroof and cranked up Yo Gotti. She sped down Interstate 10 and headed to Ben Taub Hospital with only one thing on her brain. Finding out who murdered her brother.

$$$

CHAPTER 21

"REMORSEFUL"
(JACK'S PAINT & BODY SHOP)
HOUSTON, TEXAS

Mona glanced at her watch for the umpteenth time. Flagg's aunt returned her call from the message she left on Flagg's voicemail. She explained to Mona everything she knew about the situation. Mona's hand covered her mouth when Flagg's aunt said he was riding in the car with Peewee. Guilt tidal waved over her body causing tears to race down her cheeks. Flagg's aunt gave her the name of the hospital and the room number before she hung up.

Mona took a deep breath. Now she fully understood the conversation Jack was having with the dude who owned the Escalade. It all made sense to her now. Peewee was the driver of the car she turned Fast Blacc on to. And Flagg was stuck in a coma because of her means to come up. She wiped the tears from her eyes when she saw Jack walking through the door.

"Mona, I need for you to file a mechanic lien on this car," Jack said, handing her a piece of paper with the vehicle's information on it. He glanced up and noticed she'd been crying. "Hey are you alright?"

"Not really, I need to get out of here,'" Mona told him, grabbing her cellphone and purse. "One of my brother's is in the hospital," she started walking towards the door.

"Hold up Hold up! Where do you think you're going? I just told you to do something," He said raising his voice, pointing his index finger at her.

Mona stopped, "Now is not the time Jack, real talk," she continued her way out the door.

Jack stood there with his mouth wide open watching her shapely backside move with each step. He grabbed his crotch area shaking his head, imagining himself hitting that ass from the back. Mona got into her Camry and drove straight home before going to the hospital. She wanted to get out of her work clothes and take a shower.

Her mind was in shambles. She lowered her windows completely forgetting her air condition was fixed. The hot air blew through the windows and assaulted the tears on her face, drying them quickly. Her brain was moving faster than she was driving. Mona made it to her house in no time. The damage was done. All she could do now is pray for the best. She quickly showered, dressed, and was right back out the door heading to Ben Taub Hospital to see her boo.

$$$

CHAPTER 22

"SEXUAL ATTRACTION"
(SUPER 8 MOTEL)
HOUSTON, TEXAS

Lyric drove to the Eastside and exited Federal Road & Uvalde. She made a left turn at the stop light heading to pick Amber up from Hollywood's place. They made plans to cruise through the Southside then hit up The Potato Factory on Martin Luther King Boulevard, better known as the King. But before they made it there, they ended up at the closest motel. Amber couldn't stop fantasizing about Lyric's juicy lips. And Lyric couldn't keep her eyes from traveling over Amber's body.

Their clothes disappeared as soon as the door shut. Lyric took charge and told her to lay across the bed. Amber had on her brown leather knee high strap heels. Her curves were trying to escape the leopard print see through panties and bra. She laid back on the cool bed and spread her legs wide, both feet on the floor. The smell of Gucci Bloom and Floral Chloe' mingled in the air.

Lyric crawled on top of her planting soft kisses along the way. Amber arched her back then moaned out. Lyric sat up and took off her bra. Her nipple's stood erect on her perky breast. She reached down and unclasped Amber's bra, freeing her beautiful firm melons. Lyric passionately kissed her areola's and teased her nipples with her tongue. Amber bit down on her bottom lip enjoying the pleasure. Lyric drug her tongue and coasted to a stop at her belly button. She played around for a few seconds and tugged on Amber's panties.

She raised her round bottom allowing Lyric easier access for removal. When Lyric saw her mouthwatering pound cake. She sucked in air through her teeth. Amber's coochie was smooth and sat up high like a pitcher's mound. Lyric kneeled between her thick thighs and sampled her glaze. Satisfied with the smell and honey sweet taste, Lyric dove in tongue first.

Amber gasped out from gratification. Her moans turned to falsettos. Lyric rubbed her hard nipple's over Amber's playground causing her to curve her back off the bed. She clamped her lips down on Amber's clitoris sucking relentlessly while working her tongue. She assaulted her pussy into submission. Amber lost count of her orgasms and tapped out. They laid around and conversated for a few hours.

Amber's cellphone began to ring, "Hello," she answered, stretching her body before getting out of the bed.

"Hey! I was just checking on yo ass," Hollywood said, backing into a parking spot. "I left you some food in the microwave. I'm about to head on up and see Flagg again," she explained, examining her appearance in the sun visor mirror.

"Ok thanks. I'll just hook back up with you at the hospital," Amber said, working her figure back into her tight Alexander Wang dress. "If that's cool with you?"

"Yea its cool I'll be here," Hollywood told her stepping out of her SUV.

"I'm on my way," Amber ended the call. "Will you take me back to the hospital?"

"Yea, lets go," Lyric put on her clothes, grabbed her keys and they headed out.

$$$

CHAPTER 23

"HE SAY, SHE SAY"
(BEN TAUB HOSPITAL)
HOUSTON, TEXAS

Hollywood paced the floor back and forth. The EKG monitor beeped and her high heels clacked on the hard tile. She kept looking at Flagg wondering if he knew anything about her brother's death. If not, did he have anything to do with it. She knew Flagg was recently released from prison. That alone brought upon suspicion. She'd heard stories of dudes getting out of prison trying to hit quick licks to come up. Her brain skipped to Redline when she thought about prison. She smiled at the thought of him coming home real soon. He was up for parole review in a couple of months. The door swung open snapping her out of her daze.

"What's up girl," Amber said, walking in the room with Lyric following behind her.

"Nothing just thinking," Hollywood glanced at Lyric wondering who she was.

"Hollywood, this is Lyric. My friend I told you about," Amber introduced the two women.

"Hey! How you doing?" Hollywood asked, outstretching her hand.

"I'm ok," Lyric responded, shaking Hollywood's hand gazing at her beauty and style. She peeked at the dude laying up in the bed.

"How's he doing?" Amber questioned, stepping closer to Flagg's bedside.

"The nurse said he's ok for a person in a coma," Hollywood announced, standing on the opposite side of the bed.

"You talk to Redline?" Amber asked, watching as Lyric sat down in a chair crossing her legs.

"Not yet. I'll talk to him tonight," Hollywood smiled at the mentioning of his name.

"Lyric, come over here and meet Flagg," Amber told her.

"That's the name I heard Fast Blacc say," she said, walking to the bed standing next to Amber.

"Who is Fast Blacc?" Hollywood questioned quickly, locking eyes with Lyric.

"A guy I met," Lyric admitted.

"Girl you said Bag or Fag," Amber shook her head smiling. "Are you sure he said Flagg."

"Yea I'm sure. I've never heard a name like that before," Lyric said, casting her eyes on Flagg's face for the very first time.

"Amber! Can you tell me what the fuck is going on," Hollywood stressed aggressively, looking at her and Lyric with hatred in her eyes.

"Lyric was telling me about a guy she met last week named Fast Blacc. She said she heard him hollering over the phone about killing somebody. Then she heard him mention Flagg's name," Amber explained carefully to Hollywood.

"Where did you meet him at Lyric?" Hollywood interrogated.

"At my job. We hooked up and went to my place," Lyric responded, not knowing Hollywood's real reason for questioning her.

"Do you know his real name?" They all looked towards the door as it opened.

"N'all, all he told me was Fast Blacc," Lyric said, staring at the girl holding the door open.

Mona stood with her hand holding the door ajar. "Is this a bad time," she wondered, looking at everyone in the room, especially the girl who mentioned Fast Blacc's name.

"No come in. I'm Hollywood, this is Amber and Lyric," she introduced everyone.

"I'm Mona, a friend of Flagg's," she said, staring at Lyric wondering why Fast Blacc's name was flowing off her lips.

"Hey Mona, are you and Flagg seeing each other?" Amber asked, being nosey. Hollywood was thinking the same thing.

"Yea, he's a close friend of mine," Mona told her, walking up to his bedside. She listened to them carry on with their conversation.

"Damn Lyric, you gave up the goods and you don't even know the nigga name," Amber joked, with a smile on her face.

"Like yo ass never had a one-night stand," Lyric voiced, turning her nose up at Mona. She sensed the bad vibes coming from her as soon as she stepped into the room.

"Yea, but not with a nigga name Fast Blacc," Amber said, making Hollywood smile.

"Hey Mona, did you hear anything about who shot Flagg?" Hollywood inquired, changing the conversation back on course.

"No, his aunt called and told me what happened. So, I came up here right after work," Mona told her, with a fake innocent look on her face.

"Do you know a nigga named Fast Blacc?" Hollywood inquired, looking into her eyes.

"Huh! No, I don't know him," Mona responded, thinking how she really fucked up. "But if I hear anything, I'll let you know." she exchanged numbers with everyone.

Hollywood felt something wasn't right with Mona. The way she kept looking around and frowning up at Lyric. She also kept gazing down at her watch. She couldn't stand still and only looked at Flagg twice since she'd been there. Hollywood was really good at reading people. Her intuition never led her astray.

Mona wasn't feeling the uncomfortable atmosphere flowing throughout the room. She was more pissed off at Fast Blacc for talking his business in front of a bitch he'd just met. She cut her eyes at Lyric who was still running her mouth. Mona's eyes blazed with fury. She kissed Flagg on the cheek and discreetly tried to make an exit while they were conversating. Little did she know, Hollywood was stalking her every move.

"It was nice meeting you Mona," Hollywood said, right when Mona was about to cross the threshold.

Mona stopped, rolled her eyes and forced a smile before turning around. "Thanks, I'll keep in touch," she lied, walking out the door mumbling profane language underneath her breath. She made it outside to her car. She dialed Fast Blacc's number as soon as the car door closed. She couldn't believe how stupid and careless he was.

"What!" Fast Blacc answered on the third ring with an attitude.

"You a stupid mutha fucka!" Mona barked into the phone.

"Bitch, what you whining about now" he responded frowning up his face.

"Yo dumb ass! You act like you're trying to go to jail. You running your mouth over the phone in front of a bitch you don't even know," Mona hollered, starting up her car.

"What bitch? What the fuck are you talking about?" he wondered, pulling his car over into the parking lot of Church's Chicken on Tidwell and Mesa Road.

"Lyric! She was at the hospital saying she heard you talking to somebody on the phone about killing someone," she explained, aggressively.

"That don't mean shit," he said, fishing for more information. "The dude you killed his name is Peewee. His sister was at the hospital visiting Flagg," Mona told him turning on her air conditioner.

This was his second time hearing that name within a week. "Who the fuck is Flagg?" he inquired, gazing around the parking lot.

"He was in the car too," Mona informed him, leaving out the fact that she knew Flagg. "He's at Ben Taub in a coma," she exhaled stressfully.

Fast Blacc sat with the car idling listening to Mona give him details about what happened. He reached his hand into the ashtray and grabbed the sherm he'd been smoking. He struck the lighter and touched the fire to the end of the cigarette bringing it back to life. He inhaled slowly until the filter began to burn. Fast Blacc thumped the butt outside of the car. Mona was still rattling on in his ear.

When she gave him the room number Flagg was in, he ended the call. That was all he needed to hear. His mind revolved with thoughts of casting out all threats to his freedom. The corner of his upper lip slightly raised as he pulled out of the parking lot.

$$$

CHAPTER 24

"BACK AT IT AGAIN"
(BEN TAUB HOSPITAL)
HOUSTON, TEXAS

Flagg was unaware of the unexpected visitor standing over him. The visitor stared down at him with curiosity fiddling through his mind and hatred beaming from his eyes. Why did his contractor act so angrily behind this individual he wondered? He looked at all the tubes connected to Flagg's body. The KGB monitor beeped lowly. He bent down and whispered in his ear.

"Just wanted to see who you was before I ki—!" his words ceased immediately when the door opened.

"Oh, excuse me sir! Didn't know Mr. Hunter had a visitor," the doctor said entering the room. "Hi, I'm Doctor Wilson," she greeted, holding a clipboard and pen stepping towards her patient's bedside.

"Hey, my name is Henry," he lied, eyeing the Doctor.

"Well Henry, your friend is doing pretty good. As of now we can't say how long he'll be in a coma. But he is showing signs of progress," she looked up and smiled.

"He's mumbling 254 on white shoes. Whatever that's supposed to mean," she explained, while continuing to check and log in his vitals.

He stepped closer to the bed hiding his shoes from view. "How long do people usually stay in a coma?" he asked, cutting his eyes grimly at Flagg, then looking up at the Doctor with a counterfeit smile.

"That's a question I can't answer. It all depends on him," she replied, nodding her head in Flagg's direction. "Well, I'm done here. It was nice meeting you Henry," Dr. Wilson said, placing the pen in her top jacket pocket then making her way out of the room. The unexpected visitor gazed down at Flagg.

"I'll catch you another time," he said, with his voice light. "You know a little bit too much," his expression tightened clenching his jaws. His eyes glinted dangerously as he made his exit.

$$$

CHAPTER 25

"NO TIME FOR GAMES"
(WAREHOUSE)
KILLEEN, TEXAS

T he duffel bag of weapons Ralo brought to the warehouse was still sitting on the table. Fast Blacc, Lil' Brandon and Tron sat around talking shit and getting high. The local news blared from the flat screen television.

"HI, I'M KIARA YARBOUGH REPORTING LIVE FROM THE SOUTHSIDE WHERE A BODY WAS FOUND BURNT BEYOND RECOGNITION. I'M STANDING HERE IN THE PARKING LOT WHERE A VEHICLE WAS PURPOSELY SET ABLAZE WITH A HUMAN BEING INSIDE," the news reporter announced, causing them all to dart their eyes towards the television. "HERE BEHIND ME YOU CAN SEE THE GROUND WHERE THE VEHICLE WAS BURNED. THE COUNTY CORONOR IDENTIFIED THE PERSON AS A WOMAN. HOWEVER, HER IDENTITY STILL REMAINS A MYSTERY. IF ANYONE KNOWS ANYTHING ABOUT THIS HORRENDOUS CRIME, PLEASE NOTIFY THE LOCAL AUTHORITIES. THERE IS A TEN THOUSAND DOLLAR REWARD FOR ANY LEADS TO AN ARREST. THANK YOU!"

Tron was the first one to speak, "That's why them laws had the street blocked off the other day," he gazed at Lil' Brandon with his face unreadable.

"That sounds like some shit Ralo would do," Fast Blacc laughed, opening a fresh pack of Newport short cigarettes in the box.

"I wouldn't put nothing pass that nigga. Ralo be on some more shit," Lil' Brandon voiced, right when the steel door creaked open. "Look what the wind blew in," he said lowly, as Ralo walked through the door.

"What you nigga's talking about," Ralo barked, with murderous eyes locked on Tron. He finished up the sherm he was smoking and dropped it to the floor stomping it out with his feet.

"About the bitch they found burned up behind the warehouse," Tron vexed, matching his non intimidating stare. "Sounds like some shit you'd do."

"So, you niggas up in here gossiping like some bitches huh," Ralo said, looking back behind him. "Didn't I tell yo bitch ass to stay in the car," he hollered out, pushing at the air with his hand.

Fast Blacc shook his head gazing at Lil' Brandon, who was making the crazy sign with his index finger circling around his ear. Tron blew air through his lips and ran a hand over his face.

"Who you talking to man?" he asked with raised eyebrows.

"Niggas what! What the fuck you talking about!?" Ralo yelled at the top of his voice. "Shut yo bitch ass up," he screamed at the invisible person behind him. "You niggas think this shit is a game huh!" he reached under his shirt and pulled out a .9mm from the waistband of his jeans. "Oh, ain't nobody talking and laughing now huh! Bitch ass nigga's!" Ralo roared like a drill sergeant pointing the gun in their direction.

Lil' Brandon moved closer to Tron's shoulder with his voice low, "What you wanna do?"

"Just chill," Tron told him, gazing at Fast Blacc who was staring at Ralo with cold eyes.

"Fuck that white bitch! She talked too fuckin much anyway," he said loudly, leveling the gun directly at their faces. "That's why I killed and burned that bitch up. Fuck that hoe!" spit flew out of his mouth as he yelled.

$$$

Bug pulled into the parking lot of the warehouse. He placed the big white 750i in park then push stopped the engine. When he opened the car door, he instantly heard someone yelling from inside of the building. When he approached the door the voice became distinct. Bug peeked through one of the grimy windowpanes and saw Ralo's silhouette. He inched open the front door carefully.

Ralo's voice boomed from within, "None of you bitch ass nigga's got nothing to say huh!" the .9mm he waved in his hand had everyone in check.

A slow smile crawled across Tron's face when he saw Bug sneaking up behind Ralo.

"What the fuck you smil—!" those were Ralo's last words before he collapsed down to the cold concrete floor. Bug introduced the butt end of his .45 automatic to the back of Ralo's skull.

Lil' Brandon jumped up and grabbed the pistol that laid next to Ralo, "I don't know about them. But my prayers were answered," he voiced sincerely.

"What happened?'" Bug demanded, shaking his head side to side slowly. He felt vicious about what occurred. Him and Ralo were good friends. But the situation he witnessed had to be suspended.

"That stupid mutha fucka tripped out," Fast Blacc spoke out, casting deadly eyes down at Ralo.

"He came in while we was talking about what happened behind the warehouse. The bitch on the news said a hoe was found burned up inside," Tron explained, to his cousin Bug. "I told the nigga that sounded like some shit he'll do. He got to hollering and talking to hisself and pulled a gun out on us," Tron sat back down on the couch and blazed up a Black &c Mild.

Bug stood there with his mind registering everything he'd witnessed and absorbed from the crew. "Y'all help me put this nigga in his car," he ordered, placing his gun back into his waistband. "One of you nigga's follow me to his grandma's house so I can drop him off," he bent down and grabbed ahold of Ralo's legs.

Tron and Fast Blacc each pulled him up from underneath his arms. Lil' Brandon held the front door ajar, then ran and opened up the passenger's door to Ralo's car. He raised the seat forward and they maneuvered his body into the backseat of the Cutlass.

Tron got into his car and followed Bug to Ralo's grandmother's house. Bug parked the car in the driveway and left the window cracked. He placed the car keys back into Ralo's pocket then closed the door. Bug wanted to inform Ralo's grandmother that he was in the car. He quickly ignored the thought, because he knew he'd be there all night explaining to Mrs. Mae what had happened. He hopped into the car with Tron and they drove off.

Bug's conscience irritated him. He felt like he'd betrayed Ralo's friendship. Loyalty meant a lot to him. But when the barrel of a gun is pointed at someone you were raised up with, all loyalty goes out the window. Blood is thicker than bullshit any day.

$$$

CHAPTER 26

"ANOTHER DAY CLOSER TO FREEDOM"
(GLASS HOUSE)

Redline sat in his cell jamming 97.9, The Beat, on his homemade paper speaker. The sounds of Yellow Beezy bounced off the concrete walls of the 5 by 9 cell. He peeped at the time on his clock radio which displayed 11:15am. He began getting ready for his every Saturday visit. Hollywood showed her love and loyalty to the upmost. She traveled 6 hours round trip 4 times a month, 48 times a year, for the last 4 years. Seeing her beautiful face and being able to hold her in his arms made the years fly by.

He reached underneath his mattress and grabbed a pair of ice white clothes. He slipped into the pants and slid the shirt over his fresh white T shirt. He strapped up his snow-white Reeboks and tucked in his shirt. A prison rule. He dabbed some Dolce & Gabbana light blue oil in the palm of his hand then rubbed his hands together rapidly. Once the oil heated up, he massaged it on his skin and stroked it over his clothes. He looked at his reflection in the mirror while brushing his hair. The face staring back nodded its approval. An uneven smile tip toed across his face as he rubbed a hand over his waves.

Redline gazed at the time again...11:45am. He knew Hollywood always showed up at 12:00pm or a little after. He poked the spy mirror out of the bars and scanned the row. The coast was clear. Big Ro had given him a piece of Wedding Cake. He hung a sheet up across the cell concealing his misdeeds. He performed magic on the electrical socket and blazed up the half of joint. One deep pull from his lungs and it was over with. He flushed the roach down the toilet. He held his breath as long as he could before blowing the smoke into the vent. He brushed his teeth, took the sheet down, and waited until his name was called over the loudspeaker for visit.

The visitation room was jam packed like always. Different scents of perfume attacked his sense of smell.

"What's your name?" an Officer named Miss Hamlet asked. "Jones!" Redline responded, showing his ID card.

She ran her index finger down the paperwork locating his name, "You're visit is in row C," she told him pointing in the direction.

"Alright!" he said, peaking at her fat round ass before walking away.

Redline saw Hollywood walk back to their table with her hands filled with snacks. Another inmate tried to steal a glance at her plump backside as she passed by. He was caught and rewarded with a slap from his girlfriend. Redline covered his smile with his hand and laughed. He didn't blame the dude for looking. Hollywood wore a pair of skintight white jeans that molded each curve. He couldn't stop gaping at the nice print between her legs. She sported a pair of heels and a black shirt with white letters on front which read, MILK DOES A BODY GOOD. Her hair was dyed blond with brown highlights flowing passed her shoulders.

Hollywood gazed up and saw him standing there looking so handsome, "You gonna stand there and look or give me a hug," she pouted, with raised eyebrows.

Redline embraced her tightly. The sweet-smelling fragrance of Prada Candy invaded his nostrils. They tongue wrestled for a few seconds before sitting down. "Girl, I wanna bend your fine ass over this table," he admitted, holding her hands.

"Well, what are you waiting for?" she asked, standing up unbuckling her belt.

"Girl sit your crazy ass down," his face flushed instantly.

He smiled at her as she sat back down. He knew she would've bent her ass over if he really wanted her to.

"Don't ask if you really don't want it," she teased, caressing his hands. It felt good to be able to hold and talk to the man who owned her heart. "Baby, I'll be glad when you come home," she voiced sincerely.

"I should be home this year. Lori Redman said I got a good chance this time," he opened up the cold Fanta strawberry soda and took a sip.

"That's what the bitch said the last two times. We should've got Tameka Soloman," she hand fed him one of his favorite chips. She bit down on her bottom lip when he stuck out his tongue. "Don't be teasing me like that," she felt the heat rush over her body squeezing her thighs together.

"What are you talking about," Redline eased the Cheeto into his mouth with his tongue. He licked his lips and smiled at her.

Hollywood grabbed another Cheeto out of the bag and threw it at him. "Adrain, you just don't know how much I love you."

Redline knew she was serious when he heard his government name. "Dychelle, I love you too," he leaned forward and kissed her hand. He changed the subject and batted his eyelids quickly before his tears escaped, "You and Amber getting along?"

"Yea, she's cool people. Plus, I needed someone to help me ease my mind. Thanks for sending her," she sucked the cheesy layer that was caked on her fingers. "I think we found out who killed Peewee and shot Flagg," she stressed unexpectedly.

"You did," he raised an eyebrow in disbelief when he heard Flagg's name. "Who was it?" he asked taking a gulp of his soda. "Some nigga name Fast Blacc," Hollywood said with anger in her voice. She popped the top on her Root beer soda.

"How do you know?" he asked, without expression on his face like a mask. His palms became damp, so he wiped them on his pants. Hollywood explained everything that occurred at the hospital.

Her thoughts on revenge raced faster than the words that were coming out of her mouth. Her brother had a bonified avenger of blood on his team. It was her duty to find his killer. It was her goal to seek her form of justice. It was her life or theirs. Murder glinted from her face. She blew air out of her lips in anger and frustration. Redline sat there attentively listening to her each and every word. His brain was in overdrive about the situation at hand.

What could be done?

What could he do?

Who could he trust?

"Mr. Jones! Your time is up," Miss Hamlet told him, snapping him out of his daze. She stepped over to the next table to inform another inmate the same thing.

Hollywood stood to her feet with watery eyes, "I love you baby," she hugged him wiping at the tears on her face.

"I love you too momma," Redline replied, kissing her tears

from her face. "I'll call you when I go back to work," he whispered in her ear before walking away.

He held back his tears. He wanted to be strong for her during her weakest moments. Back in his cell he paced the floor quietly as his cellmate lay asleep. Angry thoughts buzzed around in his brain. Redline blew air out his mouth in frustration.

If he would've only listened, Flagg would've not been in a coma. He shook his head at his own stupidity. Greed had got the best of him. He knew if he'd only did what was suggested, Peewee would've been alive, and Flagg wouldn't have been shot. All he had to do was keep things frozen until his release. But the temptation of making money defrosted his rational frame of thinking. Now he had to wait until he was free from prison in order to eliminate the problem at hand...Fast Blacc.

$$$

CHAPTER 27

"MADMAN"
(6TH STREET)
KILLEEN, TEXAS

Ralo woke up to a slow throbbing pain and a feeling of dizziness. He kept his eyes closed until his mind registered his whereabouts. Once the room stopped spinning Ralo gazed around for his Grandmother. He sat up on the couch pondering how did he get here. He rested his elbows on his knees and lowered his head. He rubbed each temple in a circular motion with his thumbs.

"You don't know shit!" he hollered out, jerking his head to the right.

His Grandmother heard him from the kitchen where she was preparing breakfast. "Ra Ra, are you alright baby?" she asked, walking into the living room to check up on him.

"Yea, I'm good Granny," Ralo said, looking up at her standing in the kitchen doorway.

"Who you in here yelling at?" she questioned, looking over the top of her eyeglasses with raised eyebrows.

"Had a bad dream Granny. How did I get over here?" he wondered, rubbing his head.

"I don't know baby. Your uncle Rick found you laying in the back-seat of your car and brought you inside," his Grandmother told him.

Ralo checked his pockets when she said his uncle Rick's name. He didn't trust the old crackhead one bit.

"Ra Ra, I don't know what you're doing out there in them streets. But, boy you need to get yourself together and go to church," she stressed, tightening up her robe and adjusting her glasses on her face. "I'm fixing breakfast baby, now go and wash up," she turned around and went back into the kitchen.

Ralo stood up and headed towards the front door. "Don't follow me! Sit yo bitch ass down," he snapped, through clenched teeth looking back. He walked outside and got back into his vehicle.

He grimly gazed at his Grandmother's house then darted his eyes to the passenger's seat. "Where the fuck you think you going," he looked into his eyes in the rearview mirror. "Don't say shit!" he started the car and reversed out of the driveway.

Mrs. Mae walked out of the kitchen with a hefty plate of scramble eggs, hash browns, bacon, grits, strawberry preserve and toast in her hands. "Ra Ra, your breakfast is ready," she yelled out, thinking he was in the bathroom. When she didn't receive an answer back, she casted her gaze out the front window and saw Ralo's car was gone. She shook her head and prayed to the Lord for his protection. She made the sign of the cross over her body then walked back into the kitchen.

Ralo parked his car in front of his safe haven. A burned down abandoned house. An old war veteran killed his wife, kids, dog, and then set the house on fire before blowing his brains out. The yellow crime scene tape still surrounded the house. Ralo jumped out of his car with his sweeping gaze locked on his surroundings. He ducked under the yellow tape and pushed the front door open.

The scorched smell wafted through the air. He stepped over the burned debris and sat down on a milk crate. The chalk outline of the dog and the two children were still visible on the charred black floor. Ralo bent over and removed a few planks away from the floorboard. He reached underneath the floor and pulled out a camouflage duffel bag. The bag was filled with more stolen arsenal he'd got from Mellissa. He opened the bag and selected a grenade and two pipe bombs. He sat the duffel bag back under the floor and replaced the planks. He walked over to the corner of the room and picked up an old Folger's can and sat back down. Inside the can was a pack of Newport's and a couple $100 bottles of Gorilla Piss. Ralo soaked a cigarette all the way to the filter and blazed it up.

"You ain't getting none of this. You can't handle this shit!" he said to himself, smacking his lips together with pleasure.

He sat there and enjoyed the astounding drug on the market as it took control over his brain. "I said no bitch!" Ralo yelled out, inhaling deeply looking over his shoulder grimly.

$$$

CHAPTER 28

"THE NEXT DAY"
(WAREHOUSE)
KILLEEN, TEXAS

Tron just got off the phone with the lawyer he hired. He'd wanted to make sure there wasn't any changes in their agreement. There wasn't no time for rookie mistakes. He had too much riding on the line. Plus, he was getting tired of playing the middleman. Tron glanced over at Fast Blacc and Lil' Brandon battling it out playing Call of Duty.

"Hey! Ain't none of you nigga's seen Ralo?" Tron inquired, thinking back to the incident yesterday.

"N'all, He probably still sleep," Lil' Brandon joked. "As hard as Bug hit his ass," he laughed.

Fast Blacc shook his head, "If anybody seen 'em it'll be Bug. You think he might trip out when he shows up," he asked, gazing back at Tron.

Right when Tron was about to respond to the stupid ass question, Bug walked in with three young slut buckets. Each one had a fat butt and a fat coochie to match.

"What's jumping in this bitch," Bug voiced, shaking everybody's hand.

"I know what's about to be jumping," Fast Blacc stressed, rubbing his hands together. "Say lil' momma, come sit your fine ass down," he said, patting his hand on the couch.

"Boy, you don't even know me!" the one named Shakira snapped, placing a hand on her hip.

"Once you sit down I will," Fast Blacc grilled her, showing off the platinum and diamonds in his mouth.

"I guess so," Shakira strutted her way and sat down next to him on the couch. Her homegirls followed suite and got in where they fit in. Lil' Brandon threw a sack of Berry White Kush on the table for them to roll up.

Tron pulled Bug to the side to find out if he'd heard anything from Ralo. They both knew Ralo was a problem that had to be dealt with sooner or a later. Bug didn't want to think about it. He knew he'd be the one putting in the work. He shrugged away the unwanted feeling and went to join the smoke session.

$$$

Ralo controlled the steering wheel with his left hand. He held the grenade in his right hand. He raised the pineapple to his mouth, removed the pin with his teeth and spit it out the window. He recklessly turned down the street where the warehouse was located at. One of the pipe bombs slid off of the passenger's seat onto the floorboard.

"See what yo stupid ass done. I outta put yo bitch ass out," Ralo grabbed the grenade with his left hand and controlled the steering wheel with his wrist. "Get yo bitch ass out the way," he slapped the empty seat and reached down to grab the pipe bomb off the floor.

He leaned a little further and grasped the bomb. When he raised up and looked. His eyes widened. Ralo crashed into the back of a parked truck on the side of the street. His head slammed against the steering wheel. He looked around dumbfoundedly before coming to the conclusion that the grenade was no longer in his fist. When his gaze finally locked in on the grenade that rested on the floor between his feet...it was too late.

$$$

The explosion blew out the front windows to the warehouse.

Everyone dove down to the floor until the tin building ceased shaking. Bug and Fast Blacc were the first two out the door, pistol's in hand, ready for war. They saw a car upside down burning uncontrollably.

"What the fuck!" Tron said, with confusion painted on his face.

The girls stood behind them with their eyes wide and eyebrows raised. Lil' Brandon walked as close as the blaze would allow him. He looked down at the smoking license plate and kicked at it. His mouth gaped, "Bug!" he hollered out, eyes glued to the ground pointing with his index finger.

Bug walked up beside him and saw what he was pointing at. It was Ralo's license plate. The word SHERM was burned badly but readable. His chin dropped down to his chest and he shook his head side to side. Bug called 911 and told everybody to go back inside. He caught the smirk Fast Blacc wore on his face. He peeped the sneer Tron displayed on his. Lil' Brandon still had a shocked expression on his feature. Bug glanced at the car again then followed everyone else inside the warehouse.

$$\$\$\$$$

CHAPTER 29

"AVENGER OF BLOOD"
(FIRST COLONY HOMES)
SUGARLAND, TEXAS

Lyric showed Amber the sex flick her and Fast Blacc made together. Amber had her eyes glued to the big black dick plunging in and out of Lyric's pretty pussy doggy style. Her juices made the fat cock shine as she backed her ass up matching his strokes. Her moans poured out of the surround sound speakers. Amber licked her lips as the black stud held onto Lyric's small waist fucking the shit out of her. Lyric turned around and wrapped her plump lips around his thickness.

"Damn bitch! You a fool on that dick too," Amber eyed her smiling.

"Bitch shut up," Lyric told her laughing, as Fast Blacc's face popped into view.

"Lowery Mitchell!" Amber said, peering at the screen closer. "What!" Lyric responded, curiously.

"That mutha fucka use to jack off every time I passed by his cell," she told her, paying close attention to his scrumptious looking dick as it exploded in Lyric's face. She didn't tell Lyric how she used to stand there and watch him masturbate until he ejaculated.

"You know him then," Lyric voiced, turning off the television.

"Lowery Mitchell," she said, rubbing the bridge of her nose.

"Yea, I didn't know his name was Fast Blacc though. I'm finna call

Hollywood and tell her what's up," Amber followed her out of the bedroom into the entertainment room. She sat down on a huge black leather bean bag.

"You wanna call that girl Mona to see if she can recognize him," Lyric handed Amber a small bottle of Moscato from the mid-size refrigerator next to the bar. She twisted open the cap and took a sip. "I think she knows something the way she kept frowning up at me," Lyric sat down on the other matching bean bag drawing her legs underneath her.

"I don't care it won't hurt. I'll call the bitch after I tell Hollywood to come over," Amber downed her bottle of Moscato then winked her eye at Lyric. She grabbed her cellphone and dialed Hollywood's number.

"Hey girl!" Hollywood answered on the first ring.

"'I'm over here at Lyric s house. You need to come over here so you can see this nigga Fast Blacc."

"Ok, I'm almost in Houston now. I'm just getting back from visiting Redline. Text me the address," Hollywood voiced.

"Alright, we're gonna call Mona over too. Just in case she can help us out," Amber told her, blowing a kiss at Lyric.

"That's cool. See y'all when I get there," Hollywood ended the call.

Amber texted Hollywood Lyric's home address then called Mona. She informed her what was jumping. Mona agreed to come over. Not to help them out, but to investigate and see what they really knew about Fast Blacc.

Lyric stood up and grabbed Amber's hand and pulled her back into the bedroom. They peeled off their clothes and explored each other's body until their fingers and tongues were exhausted. They showered, got dressed and waited to see who would arrive first.

$$$

Hollywood turned into First Colony Homes with admiration covering her facial features. The landscaping and scenery were breathtaking. She peered at the Global Positioning System (GPS) and made a right turn at the stop sign. Kids were chasing ducks along the lakeshore as parents watched on attentively. Hollywood made a right turn at the next stop sign, drove down six houses and turned into Lyric's driveway. The huge red brick home was immaculate. She got out of her SUV and stepped up the walkway.

$$$

"Hey, you think Mona's gonna show up?" Lyric asked, as they sat down at the kitchen table snacking on a bowl of green grapes.

"Yea, she probable thinks you're fucking Flagg too," Amber joked, biting down on a grape causing juice to squirt in Lyric's face.

"Damn bitch!" Lyric laughed, wiping her face as the doorbell chimed. "Hollywood or Mona?" she asked, walking to the door pulling her shorts free from her hungry butt.

"Hollywood!" Amber answered, as a smile tugged at her mouth. She reached to grab some more grapes and missed the entire bowl watching Lyric's ass jiggle.

Lyric opened the front door and smiled, "Hey girl come on in," she greeted, stepping aside allowing Hollywood to enter her domain. Lyric was captivated by her natural beauty.

"This is a nice house," Hollywood complemented, slipping off her heels without being told.

Lyric raised an eyebrow and nodded her head at that move. She was so used to asking whoever visited to remove their shoes. "Amber's at the table stuffing her face full of grapes," she told her, walking back to the dining area.

Hollywood followed her gazing around at the well decorated home. "Save me a few," she looked at Amber going to work on the bowl of grapes.

"I'm trying to eat some before Lyric's greedy ass sit back down," Amber eyed Lyric smiling "How's Redline doing?" she asked, right when the doorbell harmonized again.

"He's good, waiting to come up for parole. You know I can't wait," Hollywood smiled batting her eyelashes. She turned and saw Lyric talking to Mona standing in the foyer. Her girlish expression transformed instantly. Her eyes became bright with grimness. She peered at the sparkling piece hanging from the end of Mona's necklace.

Amber noticed the drastic change in her persona. "Hollywood are you alright?" she questioned, with a puzzled look on her face.

Hollywood didn't respond. She walked right up to Mona, "Where did you get that chain from bitch?" she demanded, balling up her fist with evil thoughts floating around her mind.

Mona evaluated the situation promptly. Three against one. The odds weren't in her favor. She wasn't scared to get her scrap on at all. But she wasn't a dumb bitch neither. "What are you talking about? If y'all are having problems I can come back another time," she voiced, trying to ease her way back out the front door.

Lyric kicked the front door closed then locked it, "Answer the question bitch," she snapped, inconspicuously grabbing an old miniature bat she got from Astroworld theme park.

"I been having this necklace," Mona said, sliding the gold and diamond laced pacifier back and forth across the necklace. She watched as Amber got up from the table and stood next to Hollywood. "It's not even real. They sell them everywhere."

"I bought that piece and chain for my little brother Peewee four years ago. I paid fifty thousand dollars for it. Its twenty-four-karat solid gold. I had his name engraved on the handle of the pacifier," Tears swiftly flooded her eyes.

"I-I don't know—what you're talking about. I'm finna go," Mona slurred, as panic coursed through her. She turned around and reached for the doorknob. Lyric crashed the bat into her face with brute force. Mona dropped to the floor.

"Hooome run!" Lyric yelled out, with a hand cupped over the side of her mouth.

"Where did you meet her at?" Hollywood smiled, wiping blood from her face.

"Bitch y'all are crazy," Amber said, casting her gaze from Lyric to Hollywood. "What are we going to do with her?"

"Beat her ass until she tells us who killed my brother. And where she got this chain from," Hollywood reached down and removed her brother's necklace from around Mona's neck. She checked her pulse to make sure she wasn't dead. "Bitch!" Hollywood kicked her in the ribs.

"Here you go," Lyric threw Hollywood a roll of grey duct tape. "Amber, I love this girl already. Help me tie this bitch up," Hollywood held Mona's legs up while Amber secured her ankles tightly. Hollywood taped up her hands and placed a piece of tape over her lying ass mouth.

"Amber, y'all drag her down here," Lyric opened a door and turned on the lights. She walked down the stairs into the basement.

Hollywood stood bent over with her hands on her knees for support. She shook her head at Amber and they drugged Mona down the stairs. Her head slammed against each step all the way to the bottom. They heaved her into a chair and tied her down. Hollywood and Amber flopped down on a couch breathing heavily. Lyric headed back upstairs to clean up the blood in the foyer.

$$$

Fast Blacc had called Mona twice and she didn't answer. He hopped on US 59 South and headed to Sugarland, Texas. He wanted Mona to help him get rid of Lyric. He fired up a sherm to get his mind right. He thought back to the conversation he had over the phone. He tried to recollect if he'd said anything incriminating. He inhaled slowly, filling his lungs with motivation. The marvelous gateway drug enhanced his wicked way of thinking. The thought of killing Mona crossed his mind again. Would she ever try to double cross him? Would she slip up and run her mouth like Lyric did? He didn't have to worry about Ralo's crazy ass. Lyric was a dead bitch in the making.

Fast Blacc lowered his sound system when he turned into First Colony Homes. Finding her house was simple. A left turn at the first stop sign, then a right turn at the next one.

"Dirty bitch!" he said, spotting Mona's car parked in Lyric's driveway. "Fuck!" he cursed out when his tire scraped the curb. He made the block and parked at the end of her driveway, blocking all the cars in. He sat there and patrolled the scene waiting for the right time to make his move.

$$$

Hollywood stood over Mona staring down at her grimly. She bent down and opened the mini fridge that sat next to her. She grabbed a beer and shook it up. Hollywood held the beer right under her nostrils and popped open the top. The beer gushed right into her nose.

Hollywood slapped Mona back to her senses, "Welcome back bitch," she sneered, slapping her again, then again, then again.

"I'm glad you not my pimp bitch," Amber said, shrugging her shoulders at the sight of Mona's abnormal face. The right side of her face was swollen, and her eye was completely shut. The big gash across her eyebrow was caked with dried up blood.

"Where did you get my brother's chain from?" Hollywood barked, swinging a hard-right cross to her chin. Mona toppled over and her head pounded against the concrete floor.

Lyric walked back down the stairs holding an iron in her hand, "This should make the bitch talk," she plugged the iron into the electrical outlet and sat in on top of the mini fridge. "Hey I'll be upstairs if y'all need me," she went back upstairs to finish cleaning up any traces of blood.

Mona started struggling against the restraints that held her bound. Her eyes casted invisible bullets into Lyric's back as she walked up the stairs. She made a silent vow to herself. If she made it out of this situation alive, she wasn't going to do anything illegal again. Mona cursed Fast Blacc again for being a dumb tender dick ass nigga. Here she was, staying down by keeping her mouth shut, and he was nowhere to be found. She kicked at the restraints again when Hollywood picked up the steaming hot iron.

$$$

Fast Blacc hopped out of his car as soon as the woman across the street went inside with her hairless cat. He walked up the S curved sidewalk without hesitation. He peered around casually before pressing the doorbell. He removed a gun from the small of his back and held it down low in front of him.

Lyric opened the front door. Her facial expression flip-flopped from curiosity to fear really quick. She threw up her hands in horror then tried to close the door. Fast Blacc bolted through the door with his gun leading the way. He grabbed Lyric around her neck and kicked the door closed. He held her against the wall and rubbed the pistol against her lips. She trembled at the touch of the cold blue steel.

"Where's Mona at?" he asked, looking around with a murderous profile.

"She's in the basement," Lyric cringed when she felt the gun between her legs.

"Who else is with her?" Fast Blacc asked above a whisper, brushing his lips against her ear. "And don't lie to me bitch!" he raised the gun upwards between her legs.

Lyric gasped out then mumbled, "Amber and Hollywood," she turned her face away from him.

"Show me where they're at," he grabbed her by the face and pushed her away. He watched carefully as Lyric walked towards the basement. Her butt cheeks were on full display peeking from the bottom of her shorts. He shook the distraction away from his thoughts.

Lyric opened the door and the murmur of conversation rose and fell. He pressed the gun into her back and followed closely behind her as she marched down the steps.

"Amber take the tape off her mouth," Hollywood commanded, holding the iron with a firm grip.

"AHHH!" Mona yelped out, when Amber snatched the grey duct tape away from her mouth.

"Who killed my brother? This is my last time asking you bitch," Hollywood was in motion within inches away from melting Mona's face.

Fast Blacc's heart thumped in anticipation as they made it to the bottom step. "Back the fuck up!" he yelled, startling everyone in the room. "Miss Stacks, what the fuck are you doing here?" he shoved Lyric in the back causing her to stumble to the floor. "Untie her Lyric," Fast Blacc ordered, contemplating his next move.

"About time yo ass showed up," Mona voiced angrily. She thanked the Lord for answering her prayers. As soon as Lyric removed the last of the tape from around her ankles. Mona stood up and connected a straight jab to Lyric's chin, knocking her completely out.

Fast Blacc saw Hollywood attempt to be a hero, "Don't even think about it bitch," he aimed the .9mm at her face. "Mona, tie Miss Stack's ass up first," he pointed with his other hand.

Mona worked fast. She had Amber tied up to the same chair she was held prisoner in for the last 2 hours. Hollywood looked on with her blood boiling as Mona used the last of the duct tape and slapped it over Amber's mouth with an ugly smile on her face. She darted her gaze at Fast Blacc who was watching her with cold eyes. Her mind jumped to Redline.

She really needed him right now. "Take your clothes off bitch," Fast Blacc hollered out suddenly.

His cold eyes quickly changed into fury. "We ain't got time for no bullshit," Mona told him. "Just shoot these bitches and let's go," she suggested looking upside his head.

"Just do what the fuck I tell you to do ok," he yelled, pointing the gun in her face. "Ok?" he stressed again, watching as Mona nodded her head up and down. "Find something and tie this lil' bitch up with. When you finish take the hoe to my car and throw her in the back so I can get rid of her," he directed his aim back at Hollywood who was moving at a turtle's pace taking off her clothes.

Mona snatched the cord off the iron and a lamp sitting on the table. She tied Lyric's hands and feet. She peeked at Hollywood removing her clothes and saw the sick perverted lustful look etched on Fast Blacc's face. As a woman she felt bad for Hollywood, even after the punishment they put her through. She picked up Lyric as if she weighed nothing and threw her over her shoulder.

"Fuck that hoe nigga let's go!" Mona told him heading up the stairs.

Fast Blacc ignored Mona's comment as his manhood began to swell in his pants. Hollywood worked her jeans down over her shapely hips. The sight of her fat pussy and wide gap between her legs caused him to get excited. "Take everything off," he stepped closer and rubbed the gun over her 34DD's.

His eyes smiled when she freed her good-looking breast. Her body was flawless, and she was beautiful. "Take off your panties and lay down," he unbuckled his belt and undid his pants with one hand. His dick jumped out his boxers dripping with precum.

Amber closed her eyes not wanting to witness something so sickening as rape. She moved around against her restraints to no avail. She also prayed to GOD for help.

Mona came back down the stairs and couldn't believe what she saw. She stood there in shock. She knew Fast Blacc was crazy, but she never knew he was sick in the head. "Nigga, what the fuck are you doing? We gotta go! A white lady saw me put her in the car," she lied, hoping it'll change his mind.

"Here I come. Go get in your car," Fast Blacc told her, changing his premeditated sick minded plan. He swung the end of the .9mm down on the top of her head knocking Hollywood unconscious.

He fixed his clothes and ran up the steps by 3's. He closed and locked the door. His eyes registered on the bar in the entertainment room. An ideal popped in his head. He went and grabbed two bottles of liquor and walked back into the kitchen. He grabbed a towel off the counter and tore it into two strips. He poured out a quarter of each bottle and stuffed the strips of cloth down into the liquid. He lit the first cocktail bomb and slammed it against the basement door. It exploded upon contact. Flames spread quickly over the door and the walls. He lit the next cocktail and threw it against the bar, breaking other bottles causing a small explosion. He made his escape without appearing suspicious. He calmly closed the door and walked to his car. His eyes peered around at his surroundings and noticed no one around. He hopped in his car and drove away with Mona tailing him.

$$$

Amber smelled something burning well before she witnessed the thick white smoke creeping down the stairs. Hollywood was still laying across the couch naked and unconscious. Amber began rocking the chair side to side like Mona did. She muffled out Hollywood's name thrashing around in the chair. The thick heavy smoke snailed closer to the bottom of the stairs. Amber wildly maneuvered her body inching closer and closer towards Hollywood. Her mind yelled out Hollywood's name as loud as it could. Amber nudged her body against Hollywood's leg over and over.

The smoke settled heavily and begin to worm into her nostrils. Hollywood started coughing uncontrollably as the fumes raped her lungs. When her vision focused and her brain acknowledged what had happened, she quickly sat up. Her hand darted straight between her legs and examined her goods. She felt something bump against her leg and looked down. She peeled the tape away from Amber's mouth.

"Hurry up and get this tape off me girl. I think the house is on fire. We gotta get out of here," Amber said between coughs.

Hollywood searched for her clothes at a slow pace. She was still shocked at awaking naked against her own free will. She slid back on her panties and bra.

"Girl hurry up. He didn't do shit," Amber said, noticing the grilling look on her face. "Your pants are under me. Hollywood hurry up please," the smolder clouded the entire basement.

Hollywood squinted her eyes as the fumes engulfed them. She swiftly freed Amber from her restraints. She felt the big lump on the top of her head and her face registered pain. Amber ran up the stairs holding a towel over her mouth and nose. She reached for the door-knob and was rewarded with pain. She hollered out as the heat sizzled her palm. She turned about and fled back downstairs.

Hollywood reached for a ball off the pool table and pitched it like Cole for the Houston Astros. The six ball shattered the window. Amber grabbed a pool stick and began knocking the glass away. Hollywood sat the chair Amber was occupying on top of the couch. Amber held the chair steady until Hollywood made it outside. Hollywood leaned back inside the window and helped her to safety.

The house was ablaze. They both limped and hobbled to the front of the house. The glass from the window cut into the bottom of their feet. Hollywood looked up at the blazing fire and jumped into her SUV. Amber didn't have to be told what to do. Her door closed before Hollywood opened hers. Hollywood backed out of the driveway and drove into the night.

$$$

Fast Blacc was en route straight to Killeen, Texas. His eyes traveled back and forth at each mirror for the past 30 miles. He wanted to make sure no one was following him besides Mona. He picked up his cellphone and called her.

Mona answered on the first ring, "Yea, where the fuck we going?"

"Lookout Mona don't worry about a mutha fuckin' thing. I got everything under control, you hear me?" he explained, as his eyes danced from the rearview mirror to the road. Mona listened as he explained his plan.

Lyric laid bound by a cord in the backseat. She quietly listened as Fast Blacc talked on the phone while she swiftly and calmly worked on loosening the restraints.

"Just keep following me. I got a spot out in Killeen where we can get rid of the bitch," Fast Blacc said, ending the call.

He wiped the sweat away from his head with his forearm. He held the steering wheel steady with his left knee. He reached for the vanilla extract bottle filled with formaldehyde. Fast Blacc inserted a More cigarette into the clear substance. The smell quickly invaded Lyric's nostrils. She tried to blow the fumes away. The formaldehyde drowned all hopes of clean air.

Mona trailed behind Fast Blacc with only one thing on her mind... fucking Lyric up. Mile after mile different ways to torture her acrobated across Mona's consciousness. She glanced at her reflection in the rearview mirror and didn't recognize the person gazing back. Her face was swollen, battered, bruised, and gashed. Mona looked like the elephant man's sister. She snatched the rearview mirror down from the windshield and threw it against the dashboard.

"I'm gonna kill that bitch," Mona pounded on the steering wheel with her fist. She peeped the highway sign, 67 miles to Killeen. A sluggish grin unfolded across her feature. She set the cruise control on 75 mph and pursued her victim.

$$$

CHAPTER 30

"REALITY CHECK"
(FEDERAL ROAD)
HOUSTON, TEXAS

Hollywood helped Amber removed the glass shards from the bottom of her feet. It took her an hour to get the tiny particles out of her own. Little conversation was held between the two. Each one was raveled around their own deep thought. The frightening episode left a stigma on their brain.

Amber glimpsed up at Hollywood, "Girl, let me find out you like this shit," her voice broke the quietness.

"What are you talking about," she asked, looking up from her feet perplexed.

"Digging in my damn feet," Amber voiced, with tears filling her eyes threatening to overflow.

"I know it hurts. It'll feel better once I get all the glass out. Trust me, I know how you feel," Hollywood showed her the bottoms of her own feet.

"Where do you think they took Lyric?" Amber winced, as she pulled out another shard. She noticed how Hollywood took her time answering the question.

"I'm a put it like this Amber," she glared at her. "If you killed somebody and thought you got away with it. But come to find out somebody saw you," Hollywood sat the tweezers down. "What would you do to that person?" she asked, fearing the answer.

"I'll kill their ass too," Amber answered quickly, not thinking about the question she initially asked.

Hollywood positioned a foot tub filled with warm water and alcohol in front of Amber. "My point exactly," she walked lightly to her bedroom and left Amber with her own thoughts. Her mind was on a totally different level. It churned revenge...and revenge only.

Amber eased her feet into the soothing warm water. She relaxed on the couch thinking about what Hollywood asked her. When her mind replayed the conversation over again. Her eyes widened and she placed a hand over her mouth.

CHAPTER 31

"UNFINISHED BUSINESS"
(WAREHOUSE)
KILLEEN, TEXAS

Bug sat in the warehouse contemplating about all the crazy things Ralo did over the years. He rubbed the bridge of his nose then took a swallow from the half-filled bottle of Hennessy. The brown liquor left a burning trail from his esophagus down to his stomach.

He turned his head at the sudden noise from the front door, "What the fuck you got going on?" Bug asked sternly, gaping as Fast Blacc walked in with a girl tied up resting over his shoulder.

"Man, I fucked up," Fast Blacc told him, looking around to see who else was there. "I'll tell you about it hold up. Let me put this bitch in the pool," he walked off to the back of the warehouse and placed Lyric into the empty pool.

Bug inspected Mona, "You want some of this?" he offered, holding up the bottle of Hennessy. The way she was looking, he felt she needed something to ease her pain. He passed her the bottle.

"Thanks, I need this!" Mona voiced, grabbing the Hennessy turning the bottle straight up. Her face grimaced from the burning sensation down her throat.

"What happened?" Bug attempted to probe, looking at her battered face.

Mona was about to narrate the whole story before Fast Blacc cut her off. "Man, that bitch and her homegirls jumped on my girl Mona. I robbed this nigga and it got back to him. The bitch ran her fuckin' mouth a little too much. I had to burn down the bitch house with her homegirls in it," he stressed, watching as Bug cut his eyes from Mona back to him. "I didn't know where else to bring the bitch," he told him, grilling Mona heavily.

Bug felt there was more to the story by the way Mona kept shifting her weight from leg to leg. He peeped how she rolled her eyes as Fast Blacc retold his version of the story. "Are they dead?" he wondered, watching as Mona took a deep swallow of liquid courage.

"I don't know. I set the house on fire and burnt off," Fast Blacc confessed, reaching for the Hennessy.

Mona passed him the bottle, "You might need to go back and check to see if those bitches are dead. Cause if they're not, we might be in trouble," she spoke up hoping he'd agree, that way she could handle her unfinished business with Lyric.

Bug nodded his head up and down, "You wanna head back down there to see what's up," he gazed up at Fast Blacc awaiting an answer. "Mona can stay here an keep an eye on ole girl," Bug winked his eye at her. He knew Mona couldn't wait to get her hands on the girl downstairs in the pool. "I ain't got shit else to do, let's roll," Bug grabbed his Astros cap and pulled it down on his head.

Fast Blacc eyed Mona, "Make sure you keep a close eye on that bitch. We'll get rid of her when I get back," he downed the remainder of Hennessy and sat the empty bottle on the table next to the duffel bag filled with guns that Ralo stole.

"Lock the door, and don't let nobody in this bitch," he said, following Bug out the door.

Mona wasn't paying attention to anything he was saying. Her mind went straight into vendetta mode as soon as the front door slammed shut. She looked around the warehouse for something to punish Lyric with. She stepped over to the table and peeked inside the Army green duffel bag she saw Bug zipping up. She gazed around before grabbing the FN .57 pistol with a silencer attached.

The feel of the gun gave her a sense of power along with the liquor cruising through her system. She thought back to Lyric walking down the stairs with the iron in her hand. An idea slid across her mind forcing a smile on her face. She roamed the warehouse in search of a few items to carry out her plan.

$$$

Lyric laid completely still at the bottom of the empty pool. When Fast Blacc disappeared up the stairs she started working on removing the restraints. She felt the cord began to slacken which encouraged her to move faster. She inched her body around in circles struggling to get free. The bind loosened more and more each time she wiggled and strained. Her hands were almost free. Mona opened the door and walked down the stairs holding the gun. She stepped to the pool side looking down at Lyric struggling to get free.

"I been waiting to fuck your lil' ass up bitch," Mona said aggressively. She sat the gun down on the side of the pool and went back upstairs.

Lyric knew she was in trouble then. She fought against the restraints with all her strength. The cord cut into her wrists as she tried to free herself. Her hands inched closer to freedom.

"Now I got something hot for your ass bitch," Mona voiced, walking down the stairs carrying a pot of boiling hot water. The steam rose up out of the pot at a rapid pace. "Since you like to see people get burned. Let me see how your bitch ass like this," Mona grunted, throwing the boiling hot water towards her.

Lyric made it out of the restraints just in time. She rushed Mona and tackled her around the waist. Hot water flew everywhere burning them both. Lyric was to light in the ass for Mona. Mona took advantage of the opportunity and slung Lyric's petite body against the side of the pool wall. Mona attacked her with the quickness. She kicked her in the midsection. Lyric hollered out in pain. Mona reached down and grabbed a hand full of Lyric's hair with her left hand and commenced to raining punches into her face.

Lyric found enough strength and punched Mona in the stomach, knocking the air out of her. Lyric tried to kick her in the face while she had her hands on her knees gasping for air. Mona was expecting the kick. She grabbed Lyric's leg and flung her back up against the wall.

The good Lord was on Lyric's side. When she reached up for the edge of the pool side to pull herself up, her hand landed on top of the FN .57 pistol that Mona dumbly sat down. Lyric turned around with only one thing on her mind, and that was putting Mona to sleep. Lyric aimed the gun and squeezed off three quick shots. The bullets pierced Mona right in the chest. She stumbled back into the deep end of the pool half filled with dirty murky water. Mona had a look of surprise plastered on her face as she melted down to her knees, waist deep in the water.

Lyric pointed the gun at her face, closed her eyes and pulled the trigger. The bullet drilled through her forehead and she fell sideways into the murky water. Lyric wasted no time getting out of the pool. She quickly made her way up the stairs. She didn't know she was there alone. She eased open the door and creeped out. The big warehouse was as quiet as a mouse as she peered around. She smartly wiped her fingerprints off the gun and threw it by the table before dashing out the door.

Lyric ran down the dimly lit street barefooted. It was a little after 8pm. She didn't know where she was going and didn't even care. She just wanted to get as far away from the warehouse as possible. It didn't take her long to find a ride back to H-Town.

She didn't even have to ask anyone. The way her shapely ass protruded from the bottom of her short shorts; drivers were begging to take her home. After declining several rides from thirsty looking individuals. She hopped into a car with an old white man who resembled Benny Hill, thinking he'd be different. Even his old ass wanted to get freaky. He wanted to pay her to taste her chocolate pie. Lyric told herself she was through dealing with men ever again.

$$$

CHAPTER 32

"PEEPING THE SCENE"
(PAPADEAUX RESTAURANT)
SUGARLAND, TEXAS

A couple of fire trucks and a Police cruiser had Lyric's street barricaded. Bug made a prompt U-turn and headed back towards the freeway. Fast Blacc didn't want to take any chances of being recognized by someone with their eyes on hard (LOOKING AND BEING NOSEY).

They drove to Papadeaux restaurant near First Colony Mall and dipped inside. They were greeted by the hostess upon entering. She inquired their choice of seating, table, booth or the bar.

Bug glanced at the bar area and saw several flat screens lit up. Fast Blacc followed his gaze and walked towards the bar and took a seat. Bug occupied the bar stool right next to him.

The bartender approached and placed a coaster in front of each of them, "What will you guys be having?" the bartender requested, wiping down the bar.

"Let me get a double shot of Hennessy on the rocks," Bug ordered, glancing at the bartender, then locking his eyes back on the Houston Rockets game. The Rockets were getting their ass kicked by the sorry New York Knicks.

"Give me four shots of Patron. Some lime and a Red Bull," Fast Blacc stressed, peering down at his cellphone vibrating in his hand.

The number he saw instantly brought a grim expression upon his face. He sent the call straight to voicemail. The person calling was the very reason for him being in such of a predicament. He nudged Bug in the side with his elbow.

Bug glanced and saw him pointing at the other big 50" flat screen. He peered at the close caption as the words rolled up the screen. He began reading to himself.

Fast Blacc stared on as Erica Simon reported live from the scene of a recent house fire in First Colony Homes in Sugarland, Texas. He saw in the background where the home once stood. The entire house was burned to the ground. There was a pile of burned bricks that fire fighters were sifting through making sure there were no embers. Erica Simon explained there were no casualties and that the fire department suspected arson was the cause.

"Well, now you know those bitches ain't dead," Bug broke the silence between the two. He took another sip of ice-cold Hennessy.

Fast Blacc sneered, grimly looking down at his cellphone, "Yea, lets head back so I can get rid of that bitch," he slammed down the remaining three shots of Patron and chased them down with the Red Bull. "I'll be right back," he headed towards the restroom area.

Bug kept his comments to himself. His perception told him Fast Blacc was leaving out a lot of details. He finished the rest of his drink, crunching down on a piece of ice. His hand unconsciously rubbed his chin as he was lost in thought.

Fast Blacc checked each stall making sure no one was in the restroom with him. He didn't want to make any more rookie mistakes. He returned the last three calls he sent to voicemail.

"Man, why the fuck you keep calling my phone," he scolded, right when the caller answered. The person on the other end of the line took a deep breath.

He calmly and carefully selected his choice of words, "When time and a good opportunity presents itself. Be ready to die bitch ass nigga," he coolly expressed, ending the call.

Fast Blacc kicked in the restroom stall door out of anger. "Bitch ass nigga!" he barked out, staring at his ruthless image in the wall size mirror. Everyone who knew something about his current situation had to die...there were no limitations.

$$$

CHAPTER 33

"PAROLE INTERVIEW"
(GLASS HOUSE)

Redline tossed and turned all night unable to sleep. He'd laid awake thinking about Hollywood and his freedom. He also thought about what she had said about Fast Blacc. He peered at the clock noticing it was almost time for his parole interview. He jumped down from his top bunk and got ready to leave. His cellmate was asleep, so he kept the noise down to a minimum out of respect. After washing his face, brushing his teeth and hair, he put on his clothes and waited for the door to open. The he says, they say conversation began right when the doors opened. Inmates started gossiping before they even brushed their teeth.

The morning sunlight peeked through the dirty windows as Redline strolled down the runway. Nosey inmates questioned where he was going, while others interrogated with their eyes. He made his way down the stairs and straight out the cellblock door. The hallway was cluttered with prisoners coming and going different places. Some were heading back to their cells while others were headed to work. The commissary window was open, and inmates stood in line filling out their lists. Redline shook his head at two niggas arguing over a $1.15 pack of cookies. He'd seen plenty of fights for much less.

The wait outside of the parole office wasn't long before his name was called. He walked in and took a seat. A parole counselor named Miss Stypic got right down to business and updated his release information. She logged in any new data he had. Since Redline didn't have very much additional information, his interview was terminated. She told him within 6 to 8 weeks he should have an answer back from the parole board granting their decision. She wished him good luck and told him to tell Smith to come in next on his way out.

With his mind hypnotized with the possibility of making parole, the day zipped on by. He sat in the dayroom and waited for 6'oclock work call. Redline had a very good feeling this was his time to go home. He gazed around the dayroom shaking his head as inmates played homosexual games and laughed like they were happy to be in prison. His mind jumped to the first task on his list of things to do upon his release...premeditation.

$$$

CHAPTER 34

"CLOSE CALL"
(FEDERAL ROAD)
HOUSTON, TEXAS

H ollywood's eyes stared fiercely at the image of Lowery Mitchell on the computer screen, A.K.A. Fast Blacc. The look he had in his beady eyes. The twisted sneer he wore on his face. The way his charcoal black skin gleamed. His slightly bent nose.

Her eyebrows drew closer together as she bit down on her teeth mad with rage. The hatred she felt for him was beyond vindictive. He killed her brother Peewee, and he tried to rape and kill her too. Her thoughts darted back to the episode in Lyric's basement. The perverted look Fast Blacc had plastered over his face as he fondled himself, made her want to throw up. She maliciously locked her gaze on the computer monitor. Her brain revolved with several different ways of killing the sick minded mutha fucka that stared back at her.

The cellphone centipeding over the cherry oak wood desktop snapped her out of her trance. The handsome face which appeared on the screen brought a smile to her beautiful feature. Hollywood quickly answered the phone.

"Hey bae!" she looked at the picture of them in a heart shaped frame on her desk.

"What's up momma, you alright?" Redline asked, sitting on a bottom bunk in an empty cell at his work location.

"Yea, I'm ok," she lied, touching the sore knot on the top of her head.

"I saw parole today. So in about a month we should hear something back," he explained, thumping a roach off the bunk.

"Ok, I really hope you make it this time," she picked up the picture and smiled again. She took a deep breath. "Me and Amber ran into Fast Blacc again," she removed the phone away from her ear and closed her eyes.

"What! What happened?" Redline voiced loudly, standing to his feet. Just hearing Hollywood speak his name caused him to get angry. He paid close attention as she explained without cutting her off.

Hollywood told him everything except the part about Fast Blacc attempting to rape her. She didn't want him getting any more upset than he already was. She felt his anger seeping through the phone. He told her not to worry about anything 'cause he was coming home soon. But Hollywood wasn't trying to hear it. She was going to find Fast Blacc no matter what, and Killeen, Texas was her first stop. She looked at the address on the monitor and copied it down.

Redline knew he was wasting his breath trying to talk her out of anything. Once her mind was made up on something, she was bullheaded.

"Ok, just take care of yourself Dychelle. I love you," he said, feeling bad cause he wasn't able to correct the situation.

"I will. I love you too Adrain," Hollywood replied, absorbing the pain in his voice as she ended the call.

Amber walked into the kitchen and leaned over the counter. Her gaze was locked on Hollywood. "What are we gonna do?" she asked.

"We're headed to Killeen bitch. You know how to shoot a gun," Hollywood asked, getting up from her desk.

"Bitch please! I can shoot the dick off a fly," Amber stressed, without a smile on her face. "I'm from the country bitch. Crocket, Texas," she winked her eye.

Hollywood laughed. "Alright country girl," she walked into the bedroom and got two pistols out of the safe. She checked both weapons making sure they were fully loaded. "Here!" she handed Amber a baby .9mm Ruger.

Amber removed the clip, slid the slide back, slapped the clip back into place then jacked a bullet into the chamber. "I'm ready," she said, switching the safety on.

Hollywood nodded her head. "Let's go!" she placed her Charles Bronson (38 SPECIAL) in her clutch purse and they headed out.

$$$

CHAPTER 35

"NEVER SAW IT COMING"
(WAREHOUSE)
KILLEEN, TEXAS

Fast Blacc and Bug made it back to the warehouse. They peeped the front door slightly opened. Simultaneously they glanced at each other. Fast Blacc opened the door and walked in. He gazed around and sensed something wasn't right. Bug sat on the couch and powered on the television. He reached underneath the couch and pulled out a Nike shoe box top with Purple Passion Kush in it.

"Your girl must be downstairs handling her business," Bug said, gutting a Philly Blunt.

"Yea, I'm finna go check on them bitches," Fast Blacc was about to take a step and looked down and noticed the FN .57 on the floor. He cut his eyes at Bug. He swiftly reached down and scooped up the gun undetected.

"Here, dunk a sherm while you at it," he tossed him an extract bottle containing the influential colorless drug.

Fast Blacc made his way down the stairs. He saw Mona's body floating face down in the shallow water. He peeped the cord that once held Lyric bound resting on the empty pool floor. Anger tidal waved over his body right away. He smelled the barrel of the gun. The scent of freshly burned gun powder residue immediately verified his suspicion. He checked the clip and counted four bullets. One shot was still in the chamber.

Fast Blacc spun around and headed back up the stairs. Now since Mona was dead, he didn't have to worry about killing her ass. Ralo was dead too. That only left Lyric, Miss Stacks, and the pretty fine goddess he wanted to fuck...Hollywood. No one else knew anything but the individual who hired him to kill Peewee. And of course, Bug.

He quietly crept up behind Bug. "No hard feelings man," Fast Blacc triggered off two rounds neatly into his cranium. "You just knew a little too much," he watched as Bug slumped over and fell to the floor.

He skillfully disassembled the weapon and threw the shell into a pile of metal scrap at the back of the warehouse. He put the major pieces in his pocket for later disposal. He picked up the sherm off the floor and blazed it up. He grabbed his extract bottle and stuffed it in his other pocket. Instead of tearing his ass like any other smart person would have done, he sat down on the couch and got high. He smoked up the sherm and snorted up the lines Bug neatly arranged on the table. The cocaine was so good it began running through his system. Fast Blacc sniffed up one more line and went to take a shit.

$$$

Hollywood gazed at the navigation system and slowed the SUV to a creep. She opened her Louis Vutton clutch purse and removed the .38 Special. Amber followed her lead and gripped the .9mm baby Ruger in her left hand.

"That's the house right there," Hollywood pointed with her index finger. She watched as an old black woman stood in the front yard watering the grass. "I wonder who that is," she stopped in front of the house. The old woman waved at them.

Amber lowered the passenger window. "Hi, how are you doing ma'am?" she said politely, waving her hand.

"I'm ok baby," the old woman replied with a southern drawl, releasing her grip on the spray nozzle.

"Is Lowery here ma'am?" Amber asked, with a counterfeit smile on her face.

"He doesn't live here anymore baby," she used the back of her gloved hand and wiped the sweat away from her forehead. "He's probably at that damn warehouse with the rest of those hoodlums," she informed, placing a hand on her hip.

"Can you tell us where it's at please," Amber impressively persuaded her.

"Sure baby!" she voiced, then explained the simplest way to the warehouse.

Amber listened carefully as she jotted down the directions on an empty McDonald's bag. She thanked the old lady before they drove away. The warehouse was located less than five minutes away. It was the only tin building on the street just like the old lady explained. Hollywood turned around at the corner and parked on the opposite side of the street down from the warehouse.

"You ready bitch," she asked, surveying the scene clenching the pearl handle on the Charles Bronson .38 Special.

"Let's get this over with," Amber said, clicking off the safety as she opened up the door. "Leave the truck running in case we gotta haul ass outta here," she eased the door back carefully making sure it didn't shut close.

Hollywood hopped out the SUV and eased her door closed also. She held the gun down low on the side of her thick thigh. Amber followed closely with her gun tucked under her left arm as she walked. There were two cars parked in front of the warehouse. All the windows were boarded up, so it was impossible to peep through. Hollywood led the way to the side of the building. They tried looking through the windows on the side. Years of grime and dirt made it hard to see clearly. Hollywood attempted to wipe away the film of dirt. She squinted her eyes peering inside. Her vision registered on someone laying down on the floor. She signaled for Amber to come and take a look.

Hollywood jumped off the pile of wood and headed to the back of the warehouse. She poked her head around the corner to see if the coast was clear. She grasped her weapon firmly and wormed her way towards the back door. Amber looked around as the dry leaves and branches crunched underneath her feet. Hollywood turned the doorknob and pushed. The door creaked open. They carefully entered the building as quiet as possible. Amber pointed at the body lying on the floor.

"Somebody's here," Amber whispered in Hollywood's ear. She held the baby .9mm Ruger in front of her ready for action. "You smell that?"

"Yea, that shit stinks," Hollywood replied, above a whisper.

She pulled the trigger back with her right thumb walking closer to the body slouched across the concrete. "What the fuck is that," Hollywood's face frowned from the foul smell.

"Somebody been smoking that wet. I know that smell to good, my brother used to smoke that shit," Amber said lowly, looking up from the floor. She was hoping the dude who was laying his head in a puddle of his own blood, was Fast Blacc.

Hollywood glanced around the warehouse a few more times before telling Amber let's go. She was very angry that they drove almost to two hours for nothing.

$$\$\$\$$$

Fast Blacc sat on the toilet finishing up the sherm he was smoking. He started wiping his ass when he began smelling the scent of perfume. He sniffed the air shaking his head.

"I know my shit ain't smelling that good," he mumbled to himself, wiping his ass again before pulling his pants up.

He picked up the .45 magnum off the floor and quietly opened the restroom door. The sweet-smelling fragrance became stronger. He stepped out of the restroom and saw Miss Stacks looking around.

"Ain't this a bitch," he said, squeezing the trigger with a surprised look on his face.

Amber felt the bullet zip by her ear. She ducked down and fired off several shots in his direction. Hollywood dumped off a few rounds before they made it out the backdoor.

Fast Blacc popped his head up from behind an old car just in time to see them running out the backdoor. He let loose his mini cannon. Bullets slammed into everything but their target. He saw them high tailing along the side of the warehouse through the window. He swiss cheesed the side of the building barely missing them as they ran by. The sunlight peeked through each bullet hole.

Hollywood broke both of her heels running so fast. Amber was right behind her with one of her heels intact and the other one laying inside of the warehouse. They were less than twenty-five feet away from the SUV.

Fast Blacc bomb rushed out the front door with two pistols. One in each hand. He pulled the trigger on each weapon running towards the street. He saw them jump into a Lexus SUV. He stood in the middle of the street shooting at the SUV until he ran out of ammunition.

Amber and Hollywood made it to the SUV seconds before Fast Blacc came running out the front door blasting. Bullets riddled the vehicle miraculously missing them. The back window shattered, and shots pierced through the headrests. Hollywood turned the corner with her head inches above the dashboard. Jehovah must have had his hands on the steering wheel, because she couldn't see a damn thing.

Fast Blacc stood in the street with both guns smoking. It took him a good minute for his adrenaline to stop pumping and his mind to realize he was tripping with himself. He threw the guns in his car then ran inside to get his .45. He got into his car and drove away peeping in all his mirrors. He started smiling as he thought about how gangsta those bitches were. They had more nuts than a lot of nigga's he knew. He dipped off to one of his slut's houses until things simmered down.

Hollywood was speeding down Interstate 35 until Amber told her to slow down. "Bitch, we don't need to get pulled over. We got these guns in the truck and the windows are busted out," she stressed looking at Hollywood. She felt the truck slow down to a moderate speed.

"That nigga wasn't playing huh," Hollywood said, peering in the rearview mirror. She glanced down at the speed odometer easing up off the gas pedal.

"Who you telling girl," Amber forced a laugh. "We need to get out this truck," she gazed in her side mirror.

"That was already on my mind. I'ma park it in the garage," she glanced at a State Trooper car as it was passing by on the opposite side of the Interstate. "We're gonna use Redline's car and go to your room.

He might know where I stay at," Hollywood said, as their eyes met. She turned up the radio to drown out the sound of the wind whipping through the broken windows.

The music calmed her nerves and they made it to Houston safely. Hollywood parked the damaged SUV in the garage next to Redline's white Cadillac CTS. They quickly ran inside to grab a few items. Hollywood grabbed some more bullets for both of the guns. They got into Redline's car and headed straight to the Motel Room.

Fast Blacc flew around their mind like a buzzard over a dead carcass. Hollywood thought about how she was going to kill his mutha fuckin' ass. Amber thought about what Fast Blacc may have done with Lyric. They made it to the Super 8 Motel and hid out.

$$$

CHAPTER 36

"HIDING OUT"
(SUPER 8 MOTEL)
HOUSTON, TEXAS

Hollywood and Amber stayed camped out at the Super 8 Motel. Three days had passed since their altercation with Fast Blacc. They sat on the bed looking crazy, watching TV all day and ordering from Uber eats. Amber talked about Lyric most of the day and snored all night. Hollywood sat up at night planning her revenge on Fast Blacc. She monitored the camera's she had posted in and outside of her home.

The only person she saw on the screen was the mailman. A dog stopped to take a shit on her lawn, but she activated the flood lights and scared it away. She sat her cellphone down.

"How long are we gonna stay in this damn room?" Amber complained, eating the hamburger meat and pepperoni off her slice of pizza.

She sat on the king size bed Indian style watching television. "You don't have to stay. Here goes the keys to the house," Hollywood reached over and grabbed her keys off the night table and tossed them to her.

Amber moved her leg out of the way. "Bitch, I'm not leaving without you," she eyed the keys as if they were a snake. "That nigga-is too crazy for me," she hesitated, sliding the pizza box closer to Hollywood.

KNOCK, KNOCK, KNOCK, KNOCK, KNOCK, KNOCK!

They darted their gaping eyes at the door. Hollywood wrapped her hand around the .38 Special.

"Who else knows your here?" Hollywood asked, standing up pointing the gun at the door.

"Shit, nobody!" she responded, reaching under the pillow for the baby .9mm Ruger.

"Go answer the door," Hollywood told her, motioning with the gun in her hand.

"Uhh Uhhh, bitch!" Amber said, looking at the door. "Nobody is—!"

Another loud knock cut Hollywood off. She looked at Amber then nodded her head before snatching the door open. Hollywood pointed the gun right in Lyric's face.

Lyric stood outside of the door with an appalled look on her face. Hollywood pulled her little ass in the room and locked the door. Amber threw her gun on the bed and rushed over to Lyric. They embraced each other lovingly. Their tongue's danced for a good minute before Hollywood interrupted them.

"Hey, y'all bitches need to get a room. I mean another room," she laughed, walking over and giving Lyric a womanly hug. "Girl, you almost got your pretty lil' face blown off. We didn't know who you were," Hollywood said, sitting the .38 down on the nightstand.

"I'm so glad to see y'all," Lyric stressed, hugging Amber tightly again.

Lyric sat down on the bed and began explaining what she been through in the last three days, leaving the part out about killing Mona. She was so exhausted from running around; she laid back on the bed and fell straight to sleep. Amber held her close falling to sleep too.

Hollywood sat on the bed beside them nibbling on the cold meat lover's pizza. She glanced at Amber and Lyric cuddled up. She shook her head and smiled. She thought about Redline coming home within the next month. And how she had to be available when his parole officer came over to approve his place of residence. Her mind was made up. She was going back home tomorrow. Hiding from Fast Blacc was no longer an option. She was going to shoot first and worry about the consequences later. As long as she had breath in her body, Peewee would always have an avenger seeking his justice.

$$$

CHAPTER 37

"FOUL PLAY"
(WAREHOUSE)
KILLEEN, TEXAS

Three weeks later. Lil' Brandon and Tron were cooling around the warehouse. Fast Blacc was nowhere to be found. That alone left suspicion of guilt in Tron's mind. His cousin Bug was found with two gunshot wounds in the back of his head. And for someone to get that close to Bug, it had to been somebody he knew or an inside job.

Tron gazed down at the dried-up blood on the concrete were a chalk outline of Bug's body laid. The girl that was found dead in the pool puzzled him. He couldn't figure out where she fit into the picture. But one thing Tron knew for sure. He didn't have to worry about Ralo's dumb ass derailing his plans.

"Hey Tron, I'm through with this warehouse shit," Lil' Brandon voiced, reaching into his pocket for a cigarette lighter. "Ralo got killed outside. Bug got smoked right here," he pointed at the dark red stain on the floor. He shook his head then fired up a wood tip Black & Mild.

"I was already thinking the same mutha fuckin' thing. It's too many places we can cool out at, you feel me?" Tron looked at the bullet holes along the wall of the warehouse.

He also noticed the ones by the backdoor and the restroom. He had several questions that he felt Fast Blacc knew the answers to.

"Man, let's get the fuck outta here," Tron said, glancing once more at his first cousin's chalk outline.

Him and Lil' Brandon walked out the front door of the warehouse without looking back. Each one of them headed in their own direction.

Tron planned on retaliation for Bug's death. However, he had to stay focused in the bigger prize.

$$$

Fast Blacc got tired of fucking and getting his dick sucked. The slut bucket name Miesha couldn't keep her DSL's (DICK SUCKING LIPS) off of his manhood. She woke him up each morning with her professional tongue and lips wrapped around his pole. After over three weeks of freaking it was time for him to move around. Miesha had him drained and exhausted. He woke up one morning before her soft lips had a chance to perform CPR, by bringing his little man back to life. He quietly left out of her apartment and hopped into his car.

Outside in the parking lot Fast Blacc sat in his vehicle pondering over his next move. He watched the news broadcast which reported two bodies found in a warehouse on the southside of Killeen dead. There was a $10,000 reward for any tips leading to an arrest.

That alone verified nobody was talking. He started up his car and drove away. His mind registered back on his dilemma. It didn't take him long to choose his destination. He hopped on Interstate 90 to Highway 59 and headed to Houston.

He set the cruise control on 75 mph. He guided the car with his left knee against the steering wheel. He pulled out a cigarette and prepared his motivational remedy. Once the fire kissed the end of the cigarette, he inhaled slow and deep. The mind-bending substance raided his lungs instantly causing his brain to run away from reality.

In his head he became the big bad wolf on the prowl for three little piglets. LYRIC...MISS STACKS...AND HOLLYWOOD. He took another drag then turned up the sound system, smiling deviously as he traveled down the Highway.

CHAPTER 38

"FREEDOM AT LAST"
(GLASS HOUSE)

Redline received an FI-1 (A NOTICE STATING PAROLE WAS GRANTED) over a week and a half ago. All he had to do was sit back and wait for his name to be call on chain (WHERE -INMATES RIDE A BUS TO DIFFERENT PRISON LOCATIONS). Hollywood had told him a week prior that his parole officer had visited their home. So therefore, he knew everything was approved with his living arrangements. She also told him the date he was going home.

He sat on the toilet conversating with his cellie named Mustafa. His cellmate was a Muslim who was cooler than a shade tree in your grandmother's backyard. Mustafa dropped some life changing knowledge on him before his trip out into the real world. Redline paid close attention, but he already knew he was going home with hidden agendas. He left everything he had with Mustafa.

Around 1 o'clock in the morning a guard came and told him to pack his property because he was on the chain. Since Redline gave all his stuff to his cellie he was ready to go.

After a two-hour ride on the Bluebird (A BIG WHITE BUS THAT TRANSPORTS PRISONERS), the bus stopped in Huntsville, Texas. Inmates were herded off the transportation vehicle to a secure check in point. Once all their property was inventoried, each inmate was assigned a cell. Somewhere headed home while others were being reassigned to another unit.

Redline was escorted to the releasing department. The entire process took about an hour. He was issued his birth certificate and social security card, along with a bus ticket to the city he was paroling to. He was handed a set of clothes to wear. All the clothes were donated. He looked down at himself and shook his head. He sported a pair of corduroy pants and a colorful button up shirt with two buttons missing, also with a big butterfly collar. He stood in line behind fifteen other offenders and waited to walk out the door to freedom.

The sunshine beamed down on his face when he stepped outside. Redline looked up at the clear blue sky and closed his eyes. He silently thanked Jehovah for freeing him from the belly of the beast. He also asked Jehovah for the forgiveness of all his sins, and the sin he was going to commit. He inhaled a deep breath of fresh air then opened his eyes.

Hollywood was supposed to be there to pick him up. He looked around. He didn't see her; he started walking towards the bus station. Before he had a chance to entertain the thought of her whereabouts, his mind was interrupted.

"Hey Michael, can I have your autograph," Hollywood teased.

Redline smiled then turned around.

"Oh, my bad! I thought you were Michael who played on Good Times," Hollywood laughed as she hugged him tightly.

"I see you still quick with the jokes," Redline smiled, picking her up off of her feet and spinning her around. He planted a soft emotional kiss on her lips. He smelled her scent as his tongue battled with hers.

"I think you better stop. Lil' daddy getting jealous," she grabbed his rock-hard member then gave him a quick peck on his lips. "Let's go home baby!'"

Those four words were music to his ears. They walked to her SUV. She noticed his eyes scanning over her truck for the damages she told him about. The insurance company covered the repairs for her vehicle after she reported it in stolen. Redline hopped in the SUV, reclined his seat back and enjoyed his ride home.

Now that Hollywood had her man home, she could focus more on revenging her brother's death. She had help on her side, which made her feel extra confident in killing Fast Blacc. She smiled at the thought all the way back to Houston.

CHAPTER 39

"NO PLACE LIKE HOME"
(FEDERAL ROAD)
HOUSTON, TEXAS

Hollywood turned into their driveway and pressed her foot down hard on the brake. The SUV stopped suddenly jolting Redline awake. His eyelids sprung open and his head swiveled around. He cut his eyes at her then looked around again.

Redline stepped out of the SUV gazing at his surroundings. Things looked exactly the same as they did over four years ago. He followed Hollywood inside of the house. The smell of roast beef, potatoes, onions and spices marched up his nostrils. Hollywood had the Crock Pot in full effect, slow cooking to perfection.

"You got it smelling good up in here baby," Redline said, taking off his shoes heading straight towards the kitchen. "I'm so damn hungry," he removed the lid off the pressure cooker and the steamy aroma escaped heavily.

"Boy, close my damn pot and go wash your hands," Hollywood snapped, tossing her keys on the kitchen countertop. "You're not locked up no more. You gotta get back to the program around here mister," she wrapped her arms around his waist as he washed his hands in the kitchen sink.

"Ok momma!" he said in a childlike voice.

Hollywood pushed him in the back of his head playfully. "Boy, go sit your ass down while I fix your plate," she told him washing her hands.

They sat down at the dinner table and enjoyed their meal. Redline devoured his food like he was an animal. Hollywood shook her head and smiled. His plate was clean.

"Damn baby! Were they feeding you down there," she joked, taking a sip from her glass of ice tea.

"Ha Ha Ha! Yea, but not like this,'" he told her rubbing his stomach from satisfaction. "I ain't ate nothing like this in so long. Thank you baby," he picked at a piece of roast beef that was stuck between one of his teeth.

"I hope you saved some room for dessert," Hollywood said, seductively licking gravy off her finger.

"I got plenty of room for that baby," he stressed with confidence licking his lips. "I'm finna go take a good bath and a hot shower," Redline got up from the table and went into the bathroom.

Hollywood cleared the dining table and washed the dishes. When she finished cleaning the kitchen and straightening up the rest of the house, she sneaked into the bathroom. Redline was in the shower singing, sounding like he swallowed a frog. Hollywood removed her clothes and stepped into the steamy hot shower with him.

"Who sings that song baby," she asked, reaching for a towel and the bar of Dove soap.

"That's that boy Case," he said, turning around admiring her perfect body.

"Well, you need to let him sing that," she laughed, lathering up the washcloth. "Turn around and let me wash your back," her eyes stared down at the fat red piece of meat swelling between his legs.

She grabbed ahold of it and rubbed the mushroom shaped head between her wet throbbing snapper. Hollywood moaned out closing her eyes.

"I thought you was gonna wash my back," Redline asked with a grin on his face.

"You need to stop thinking and start fucking," Hollywood pulled his body into her awaiting wetness. She groaned out with gratification and leaned her head back.

Redline pushed deep inside of her. He grabbed her thick thighs and picked her up. Hollywood wrapped her legs around his waist and her arms around his neck. She grinded her pussy on his fat dick with no remorse. Her juices coated his thickness as she worked her way down to the end. She felt his manhood pulsate with each thrust. She wanted to feel his dick deeper inside of her canal.

Hollywood unlocked her legs from his waist. She watched as his pole popped out of her coochie and stood straight up. She couldn't resist the temptation of tasting his pretty glossy cock. She stroked him slowly working her tongue over the head before locking her lips on the tip. She worked herself halfway down its length before his dick begin to throb faster. She turned around and placed both of her hands on the wall and bent over. Redline grabbed her around the waist and entered her with no brakes. He slammed deep into her pussy all the way down to his nuts.

Hollywood braced her arms against the wall as Redline pounded her pussy to her third orgasm. He felt himself about to cum and pushed as deep as he could go and erupted. Hollywood tightened up her walls and milked his dick empty. She stood up with his dick still planted inside of her. When the blood subsided in his penis. Redline pulled out slowly. His chest heaved up and down as he caught his breath.

They took turns and bathed one another. They took turns and orally pleased each other. They got out of the shower and dried off. Before they finished drying off, Hollywood rode his dick to sleep on the bathroom floor. Redline was snoring as soon as his eyes closed. Hollywood laid on top of him and rested her head on his chest. She was finally happy. Her man was home. Her lonely nights were over with. But her thirst and quest for Fast Blacc's blood remained. She drifted off to sleep listening to Redline's heartbeat.

CHAPTER 40

"BACK TO BUISNESS"
(KELLY COURT APARTMENTS)
HOUSTON, TEXAS

F ast Blacc made it back to H-Town. He headed straight to Renee's spot in 5th ward. He knew as long as he had some good powder and some fire ass Kush, she wasn't worried about anything.

Renee ran her mouth nonstop. The good cocaine and the x pills had her talking like Wendy Williams. Fast Blacc stood up and pulled out his dick. Renee was still yapping until he stuck his pole in her mouth. Then she still managed to mumble something incoherent. He grabbed ahold of her face and humped until he climaxed. Renee swallowed his babies, wiped her mouth with the back of her hand, snorted another line, then started talking about the hating ass bitches who lived next door.

Fast Blacc's ears were still humming from him holding his breath until he exploded in Renee's mouth. He sat down on the couch and sparked the Kush back up. His hearing returned to normal along with his heartrate. He tuned Renee's talkative ass out. The grade A Kush seduced his mind into a relaxing sedative state.

His mind jumped back to the first day he met his problem...Lyric. She stood in the African Boutique going about her job details minding her business. He knew if his hot dick ass wasn't so horny, he wouldn't have been in this situation. The phone conversation in her house while she stood in the doorway listening and watching him. He cursed underneath his breath. Fast Blacc knew he had to find her...and find her fast. He decided to bounce back to her job to see if she went back to work. He knew he had to start somewhere. He took another drag from the cigarillo and gathered his thoughts.

CHAPTER 41

"GUILT TRIP"
(BEN TAUB HOSPITAL)
HOUSTON, TEXAS

The closer Hollywood drove to the hospital the queasier Redline's stomach became. Nervousness clenched his body brutally. The last time he saw his homeboy was before he left prison. Flagg was more of a brother than a friend. A brother he wished his mother had. A brother he loved unconditionally like Hollywood.

"'Are you ok?" Hollywood asked, studying how quiet he became in the last ten minutes. She also noticed how his face turned pale. She parked in the first available parking spot.

"Yea I'm good," Redline lied, trying to settle the nauseous feeling he was experiencing.

"Well, if not! We don't have far to go," she smiled, placing the SUV in park. "Smile baby, it's not your fault Flagg's in here," she rubbed his hand and kissed him before getting out the SUV.

They walked inside of Ben Taub Hospital side by side. The waiting area was engaged with activity as usual. Hollywood led the way towards the elevator. They arrived right before the doors were about to close. They stepped onto the elevator and Hollywood stood behind Redline with her arms around his waist. She told him what floor to press and they rode up in silence.

The doors parted on the 5th floor and they proceeded into the busy hallway. Hollywood guided the way to Flagg's room and pushed open

CHAPTER FORTY-ONE • 195

the door. They walked inside. A doctor was leaning over Flagg's body with a stethoscope listening for irregular sounds. She looked up when Redline and Hollywood stepped in.

"Hi, I'll be done in just a minute," the doctor informed, placing the end of the stethoscope over different parts of his body.

"Take your time we're not in a hurry, Hollywood responded, walking to a chair near the window. She sat down and looked at Redline standing there watching the doctor's every move.

"How long will he be like this Doc?" Redline questioned, gazing over Flagg's physically weak appearance.

"Like I told his last visitor Mr. Henry. A person comes out of a coma whenever their ready," she explained, positioning the listening instrument around her neck. "Oh, I'm sorry! My name is Doctor Wilson," she formally introduced herself. She shook Redline's hand and nodded her head at Hollywood.

"What did Mr. Henry look like?" Hollywood asked curiously, sitting straight up in the chair. For some strange reason she sensed Fast Blacc before the doctor responded.

"Dark skin, medium build, beady eyes. He had a mouth full of diamonds and a crooked smile," Dr. Wilson described Fast Blacc perfectly. "Well, enjoy your visit," she smiled before leaving the room.

Redline stepped to Flagg's bedside and looked down at him. He felt bad for not being there to have his homeboy's back.

"That was Fast Blacc she was talking about," Hollywood told him, in a low voice. "Baby, I'm gonna kill him. On everything I love he's gonna die," she promised, thinking about her brother Peewee.

"Not if I get him first," Redline told her, wiping a lonely tear before it fell down his face. "Not if I get him first," he repeated lowly.

Hollywood stood to her feet and pulled up her thigh high tan and brown Gucci boots. She smoothed out her short jean skirt and straightened her long sleeve matching Gucci shirt. Her mind replayed what Redline had said. "Not if I get him first!" She thought his comment was strange. How could he kill a person he never saw before? She shook her head at the thought.

CHAPTER 42

"OF ALL PLACES"
(FIRST COLONY MALL)
SUGARLAND, TEXAS

Hollywood and Redline faded First Colony Mall. She wanted to buy him some new clothes. His wardrobe was still fresh, but Hollywood wanted her man up to date and on point with the latest styles. They dipped in and out of different stores buying stuff like it was Christmas time. Redline felt like a little kid again shopping with his mother. Hollywood bought him everything she'd liked to see him wear. Redline carried the bags while she swiped the credit card.

"Let's stop by here baby," Hollywood pushed him into the Victoria's Secret store before he had a chance to protest.

"Damn, at least give a nigga a chance to answer," Redline picked up one of the bags that fell out of his hand. Hollywood was mobbing around the store before he sat the bags down.

"Can I help you'll sir?" a saleswoman inquired politely with a beautiful smile. She peeped Redline up and down approving his good looks and nice package between his legs.

"You might wanna ask my girl," he responded, nodding his head in Hollywood's direction. "Ain't no telling about her," he noticed the saleswoman's gaze locked on his crotch area.

"Do you and your girl go to parties together," she questioned, with her own interior motive brewing in the front of her mind.

"Yea, every now and then. Why what's up," Redline wondered, keeping a close eye on their bags.

"I'm hosting a swingers party. I was wondering-would you and your girl like to go," she admitted, admiring Hollywood, as she selected the sexiest most expensive lingerie Victoria's Secret offered.

"N'all we good," Redline said immediately, glancing at Hollywood.

"You never know. You might like it," the saleswoman stressed, licking her lips as she reached out to touch his manhood.

Redline slapped her hand away. He picked up their bags and headed outside to wait for Hollywood. He wasn't trying to be in the doghouse on his second day out of prison.

Hollywood came out of the store with a smile on her face. She glanced back into the store then turned back around shaking her head. The sales lady told her how sexy and beautiful she was and invited her to a swinger's party, which she quickly declined. She looked at Redline holding all the bags and smiled. She caught movement out of her peripheral and turned her head. Her eyes beamed in on a person sitting on a bench in the middle of the mall. Her entire expression and body language changed in a flash. She marched directly towards the individual who was unaware of her presence.

"Bitch ass nigga! I know you killed my brother," Hollywood barked, throwing the Victoria's Secret shopping bag in his face.

"I see yo fine ass made it out alive," Fast Blacc said calmly, looking around as people slowed down with their eyes on hard trying to see what the commotion was about. "Hey Line, you better come get your bitch," he snapped, as he noticed Redline right behind her.

A crowd started gathering around them as Redline grabbed Hollywood trying to calm her down.

"You know this bitch ass nigga," Hollywood spat, with confusion etched over her face. "Huh Redline!" she questioned angrily. Redline gazed around at all the nosey on-lookers.

"Just calm down, I got this," he stared at Fast Blacc with cold eyes, pulling Hollywood away from him.

"Yea listen to yo man girl and calm down," Fast Blacc smiled, sucking his teeth.

"You lucky I don't have my mutha fuckin gun. Sick ass nigga!"

Hollywood cut her eyes at Redline. She couldn't figure out why he was so cool and calm about the situation. She saw people pointing and recording the action with their cellphones.

"You need to keep yo bitch on a leash Line," Fast Blacc warned with a sneer on his face. "Before I lace her ass up on the real," he threatened, with a forceful laugh.

"Consider yourself lucky today pimp," Redline said lowly, staring at him with hatred eyes. "We'll bump heads again, trust me," he voiced, scanning the crowd before picking up their bags. "Hollywood lets go."

Hollywood mugged Fast Blacc murderously before walking away. The crowd of nosey spectators parted as she stormed by. She had some serious questions to ask, and she felt Redline had all the right answers.

CHAPTER 43

"DEMANDING ANSWERS"
(FEDERAL ROAD)
HOUSTON, TEXAS

Hollywood prepared dinner with little conversation about the incident with Fast Blacc. Her mind dissected the scenario surgically. She couldn't swallow the fact that Redline actually knew him. All the years of trust she had for him was washed down the drain. Her brother's life was taken, and she wanted answers.

Redline sat at the kitchen table enjoying his second home cooked meal. He grubbed down on a big boy well done T-Bone steak and a baked potato that took up half of the plate. He waited for Hollywood to bring up the topic about Fast Blacc. When she didn't, he felt so relieved. He didn't feel like trying to explain why he played dumb all this time. He looked at Hollywood as she ate. She gazed up and smiled.

By the time Hollywood had finished cleaning up the kitchen and taking a bath, Redline was sleeping like a baby. She looked down at him snoring lightly. Her love for him was to strong. She had devoted her life to him. He was her everything. So, by him withholding knowledge of her brother's killer, that made her Black Widow instincts kick in.

She quietly sneaked over to the artificial plant that sat in the corner of the room. She carefully pulled up the plant trying not to make any noise. She glanced over at the bed making sure Redline was still asleep. She reached her hand down into the pot and grabbed her

38 Special. She put the plant back in place and slid into bed placing the gun underneath her pillow.

Redline stopped snoring when she straddled his body. He opened his eyes and smiled when he saw Hollywood on top of him. She leaned down and kissed him. He held on to her waist as she grinded slowly waking up his little man. She inched her hand beneath the pillow and grabbed her Charles Bronson 38 Special. She pointed the gun right in his face inches away from his nose.

"I'm gonna ask you some questions, and if I don't like the answers, I'm gonna blow your face off," Hollywood said grimly, holding the gun tightly in both hands. "How do you know Fast Blacc? Did he kill my brother? And what do you two mutha fuckas got going on?" Hollywood pulled the hammer back slowly waiting for the answers to come.

Redline quickly began searching through the thoughts that bombarded his mind. He laid there realizing certain things. Hollywood was far from stupid, and love and life were both bitches. Once you stuck your dick into them, you might as well enjoy, because a nut was bound to come. It always has to end. He knew he was Hollywood's love and life...but the nut finally came...was this the end?

Having a ride and die chick does have its advantages. But when you're staring down the barrel of a gun with her tears falling in your face, its clear that mistakes are crucial. Secrecy can be deadly...love is the killer...and someone found out! (THE GUN DISCHARGED)

BOOM!!! YEAH, SOMEONE FOUND OUT...

$$$
(TO BE CONTINUED)

ALSO BY TERRANCE HOWARD

Enigmas are lethal...and emotions are fatal. However, dying by the hands of someone you're close to is the agony of defeat. Redline left prison with good intentions for Hollywood and himself. Plans don't always mean success, and Hollywood wants Redline to help her find out who killed her brother Pee-Wee. In the midst of this escapade, attempts on Redline's life have occurred.

Where others have failed, he came out alive. How long will the blessings last? Mr. Mystery and Mr. Controversy have to face off. In doing so, Hollywood will be left to face her own confrontation. She wants to find answers..and Mr. Truth has them. Will the lady seeking answers survive to reveal the truth?

OVERBROOK XPRESS PUBLICATIONS PRESENTS

THE Grudge

TERRANCE HOWARD

GRUDGE

A feeling of deep-seated resentment or ill will.

A lot of people hold grudges for many different reasons. Some take their ill feelings down with them to the grave. As for others, they carry out their resentment in a different manner. A very vindictive way to stimulate their sick minded reasons, and personal pleasures.

A grudge...have you ever held one against somebody??? A grudge...what will you do about it??? A grudge...how long will revenge toy with your thoughts??? A grudge..you never know who has one against you!!!

OVERBROOK XPRESS PUBLICATIONS PRESENTS

Dangerous
DESIRES

TERRANCE
HOWARD

Coty Cole, a young undercover federal agent with a point to prove. She was chosen by her superior commander to go undercover as a prison guard in a all male prison to obtain incriminating evidence on an infamous drug lord from Houston, Texas.

Larry Smith, aka Bull, ran a tight organization on the Northside of Houston. Even behind concrete walls and steel bars, he continued to control the streets quite impressively, as well as the drug flow in prison.

Will Coty Cole be able to stay focused and control her lustful hormones??? Or will the curiosity of her kitty Kat lead her to DANGEROUS DESIRES

CONNECT WITH TERRANCE

overbrookxpresspublications@gmail.com

[O] instagram.com/overbrook_xpress_publications

COVER & LAYOUT DESIGN
BY

A company designed with Urban Lit in mind, NubianFX combines innovative visuals dipped in melanin swag. Get Book covers, graphics, photography & more!

NUBIANFX CREATE COVERS & DESIGN

www.ingramcontent.com/pod-product-compliance
Lightning Source LLC
Chambersburg PA
CBHW071907220626
47052CB00002B/253